# SILENCE IN THE WOODS

## J.P. Choquette

# Other books by J.P. Choquette

*Shadow in the Woods*
*Under the Mountain*
*The Pact*
*Stillwater Lake*
*Let the Dead Rest*
*See No Evil*
*Hear No Evil*
*Dark Circle*
*Epidemic*

This book is a work of fiction. All persons, events and details are products of the author's imagination or highly embellished facts.

Some geographical locations in this novel are real, however liberties have been taken by the author as to specific places within the setting.

Scared E Cat Books
Cover design: Bespoke Book Covers
ISBN-13: 978-1-950976-02-7

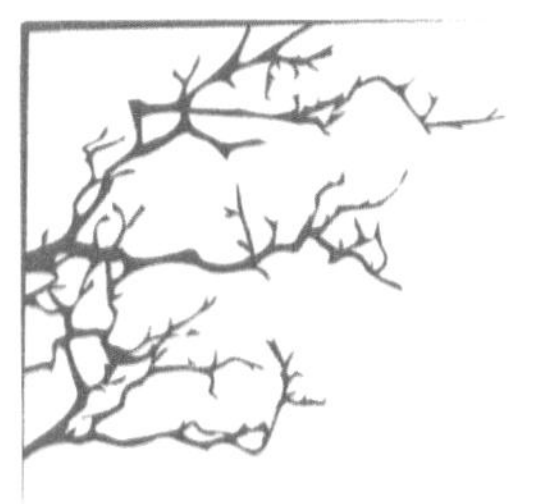# Dedication

For Serge: my one, only, always.

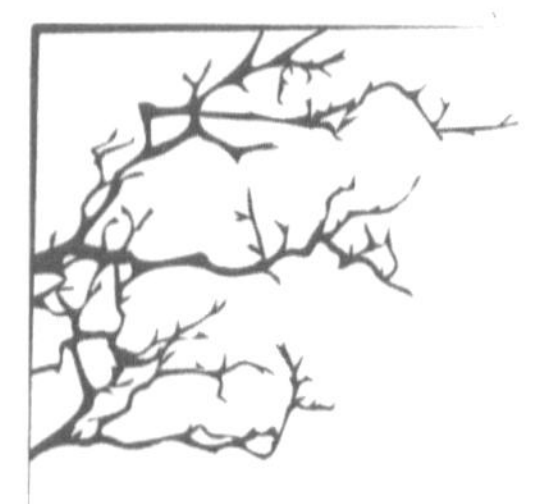

# Chapter One



*Paul Rogers*
*Friday, November 2, 1917*
*Vermont State Hospital for the Insane*

HE SHOULD BE USED TO the screams by now. Paul tilted his head, pulling the wool blanket over it, and tried to muffle the sound. The shriek rose like a wave—growing sharper and more hysterical before falling away again. Then a pause. It gave false hope: one would believe it was over. But then the high-pitched wail would begin again.

Nearby, Timmy shifted on his bed, his breath a soft whistle through his nose. Ward III was full tonight, the overflow of men spilled out into the large room next door, a hastily created Ward IV, still filled with half-cartons of supplies and stacks of old paperwork. The hospital was grossly overcrowded and Paul was lucky to have a bed at all. Many other inmates—because in Paul's mind, they were all inmates and not patients—were stuck in hallways.

Footsteps sounded in the hallway, a heavy tread. Even though Paul wanted the screaming to stop, his stomach turned. He knew who was coming.

Seconds later the man's scream ended abruptly in a bark of pain. Paul uncovered his head and lifted it gingerly in the low-lit room. A large, dark shape loomed over the bed by the far wall.

"Other people are trying to sleep, you filthy mongrel," the aide said in a raspy voice, not bothering to whisper. The man's scream had turned to a whimper.

"Quit your snottin' and shut your fat mouth," the aide said. He lifted his arm and the thump of something hard against flesh turned Paul's stomach. The whimpering died to a litany of gasping breaths.

"If I have to come in here again, I'll take you to isolation. You don't want that, do you?"

More quiet gasps. The aide must have seen the head shaking no because he retraced his path to the ward's doorway.

Paul sank back onto his bed and stared up at the spiderweb cracks in the high ceiling above. Many of the aides and nurses were kind at the hospital. But a handful was not and the night monitor for Ward III was one of these. Truthfully, it made no difference to Paul whether the other man screamed the night away or not. He hadn't slept a full night in weeks. When he'd first arrived he'd been in so much pain he hadn't been lucid. Later, after the medicines were decreased, he was able to get his bearings...and almost wished for the sweet oblivion the tiny pills had offered.

But he couldn't—wouldn't—allow himself the luxury. Whenever he closed his eyes he saw the horror he'd witnessed deep in the woods again and again. The same images would flicker, an endless loop. The two couples—he and Jane, Allan, and Deidre—and the woods, always dark and twisted, like ghostly photographs from long ago. Then the blood on the ground, a body swinging and stiff at the end of the makeshift noose—

No.

Paul sat up, putting his feet on the bare, cold floor underneath him. Timmy let out a partial giggle and Paul glanced over. The big man was so large his bulk didn't fit on the bed. A roll of flesh, soft and white like dough, flopped over the side of his cot. His face was serene, full-mooned, with his lips parted in a smile. Even in sleep, Timmy was happy and blessedly oblivious. Paul envied the big man. His childlike mind meant that he never fully grasped the harsh realities of life.

Timmy had been here for a long time. Paul wasn't sure how long, but years, decades maybe. The other inmates were a mixture of long and short-term stays. Some were here because of their penchant for masturbation, others because of devious behavior with matches or knives. Some because of melancholia or delusions. That was why Paul was here. "Delusional imaginings," were the words the psychiatrist, Dr. Hastings used. But Paul knew what they really were: memories. The mere word brought more to life: Jane's face, streaked with tears; his voice and hers screaming Deidre's name; the wild, whipping wind of the storm; the pain in his leg after he fell...

*What if we'd never gone in?* The question had spun incessantly in his mind over the past two months like a record tirelessly turning on a Victrola. What if they hadn't though? Would he be safe at home rolling onto his side in his own bed and pulling Jane close? She would nestle into him, her hair smelling like sandalwood and her skin soft and creamy. He'd been a fool to bring her on that trip. To agree to go at all. If only...

There was the second thought that never stopped rotating through Paul's mind. *If only.* If only they hadn't gone. If only Allan and Deidre hadn't been so excited about the trip into the middle of nowhere. If only Jane had caught a cold and they'd stayed home, or Paul had been called away. Instead, they had agreed with very little convincing on their friends' part.

"It will be an adventure like none you've ever had," Deidre had said. "One you'll tuck away to tell your children about." She'd painted a picture—she was a writer by trade—of an adventure so mystical and exciting that first Paul and then Jane had agreed to it wholeheartedly. If Deidre hadn't become a writer, she would have done just as well as an actress. He could see her even now, her auburn curls jiggling as she'd thrummed with excitement. It had started with the mystery of that particular piece of woods. Missing people. An unidentified animal.

Had there been misgivings on Jane's part that he'd missed? Had his excitement clouded his vision? Had it made him see only what he wanted—a grand escapade and a chance to write the story of the decade—missing entirely the doubts of his wife?

"Of course, we must go," Jane had said that blurry night when they'd been preparing for bed. Paul had overindulged in the fine whiskey that Allan had insisted on purchasing. "Only I wonder..." Her voice had trailed away.

"Yes? What do you wonder, lovely Mrs. Rogers?"

She'd stood before the dressing table, brushing her long, blonde hair. Her eyes had been far away, focused on something in the distance.

Paul had rolled off the bed where he'd been laying on his side and come up behind her. He stared at their reflection in the mirror and rested his hands on her shoulders. She wasn't delicate, his Jane, but neither was she large. Just sturdy and well-built. Her shoulders were warm and smooth beneath his hands and he'd felt a sudden surge of warmth between his legs.

"Nothing," she'd said finally. She'd smiled, put the brush to one side, and stood. She'd turned in his arms and then kissed him deeply. She had a little hitching breath that escaped her when he held her like this and he'd come to know and love it. He'd wrapped his arms around her and forgotten everything else.

Until now.

Paul stood to his feet. His right leg was healing nicely the doctor said. He pulled up his pajama pant leg now to inspect the skin in the milky light. Where the skin had been sheared off, new, pink tender skin had grown. His ankle was where the near-break had happened. When Paul had been sitting or lying down too long it still ached.

He shuffled to the open door. Here, an aide slept, slumped to one side in a straight-back chair. He was snoring softly. It wasn't the same one who'd been in Ward III earlier. Paul passed by him lightly and went out into the hallway.

The hallway was wide and long. Paul started down it toward the washroom. Moonlight streamed through the large windows, making a thick grid of squares on the floor. The iron bars in every window cast their shadows onto the floor beneath his feet. Paul thought again about Jane's unasked question that night.

What had she wondered? Had there been a premonition of what would happen in those dark, tangled woods? Had she felt a shiver of fear and chalked it up to nervousness at being out in the wild? Or had she somehow known then that not all of them would make the return trip home?

"AH, PAUL, GOOD TO SEE you," Dr. Hastings said, his voice low and deep. He got up when Paul entered the office, made a show of shaking Paul's hand, and then indicating which seat Paul should sit in. As though they didn't do this exact routine twice weekly.

Dr. Hastings was a thin, tall man who looked more like an accountant than the director of the state's largest mental asylum. He wore small glasses on his hook nose. The sunlight pouring into the room made it overly warm and a gleam of sweat shone on the man's high forehead.

"And so, how are you, Paul?" Dr. Hastings took up his normal posture behind the large desk that separated them. One leg was propped on the other, creating a writing surface for his small notebook and a perfectly sharpened pencil.

Paul nodded. "Very well, Dr. Hastings."

"Good, good. Glad to hear it. And how have the visions been?"

"Nonexistent, sir." Paul purposely kept his face neutral.

"Wonderful! That is indeed good news, young man." Dr. Hastings moved as though to jot a note on the writing pad but then stopped. He surveyed Paul over the top of his glasses. "Now, Paul, I hate to ask you this—you strike me as an honest type," he smiled a small, tight smile. "But you wouldn't simply be telling me what I want to hear so that you'll be released early, would you?"

Paul's shoulders tensed but he made a point to relax them. He looked Dr. Hastings straight in his watery, pale-blue eyes. "No, sir. I really am making good progress."

Dr. Hastings regarded him shrewdly for a moment before murmuring a, "Hmm," and scratching a note onto his pad. "And the nightmares?"

"They don't happen when I don't sleep, sir," Paul wanted to say. But that would mean explaining the trick he'd been using for the past several weeks to regurgitate his nightly sleeping tablet and all the other medications that Dr. Hastings had prescribed him.

"I still have them at times," Paul shrugged. Did it look nonchalant? "But much less frequently than I used to."

"Very good, very good." Dr. Hastings had the habit of repeating his phrases, a habit Paul found mildly annoying on a good day and teeth-clenching on a bad one.

"Sir, I believe I am well enough to be put to work. My leg has healed well and I would like to do something to pass the time. The days are long—"

"Well, we can certainly address that. Certainly address it," Dr. Hastings interrupted, peering again at Paul over his glasses. "I know they've been overworked in the laundry." His voice faded as he looked at the wall behind Paul. "Hmm, yes, that might be a possibility."

Paul's heart fell. The laundry? It would be impossible to carry out his plan from there. He needed to get into the workroom. There, the male inmates built basic furniture like chairs and small end tables. And once a week a gentleman who owned a furniture store in Brattleboro sent a truck to collect the pieces the inmates had made. Paul intended to get onto that truck, one way or another.

"That would be fine, sir," Paul said, his voice as resigned as his face felt. "Though I had hoped to be given a task in the workroom. You know, growing up my father owned a carpentry shop. I spent years assisting him and—"

"Yes, you've mentioned that before," Dr. Hastings interjected, his fingers sifting through the file of notes on the large desk. In fact, Paul's father had been a farmer but Paul had believed creating a background in woodworking would be beneficial. Apparently, not.

"Now tell me, Paul, before we get off track here—there are no more thoughts of the man-beast you saw in the woods?" The older man's voice bordered on incredulous. "It was all you'd speak of when you arrived. And yet now you say that your mental status is much improved. So improved that these delusions you had are now suddenly—" Dr. Hastings snapped his fingers together. "Poof. Vanished."

Paul tried and failed to force a smile onto his face. He wanted it to be true. Wasn't that enough? Even the mention of the thing he'd seen in the forest brought back other memories: the blood on the ground, the body swinging...the hot breath of it—that thing—on his neck. But really, what did Paul remember? That time was full of shadows, of glimpses that he wasn't sure were true. Had he seen the beast or just imagined it in his fevered state?

"No, sir. When I came here I was sick with a fever and infection. The beast I claimed to have seen was just a—what did you call it, Dr. Hastings?" Paul frowned as though trying to remember. "A delusion. An apparition created by my overwrought mind."

Dr. Hastings nodded once, slowly. "And so, Paul, even if you see images of it—this apparition—you would no longer hold onto the belief that it is real?"

Paul shook his head. "No, sir."

"Hmm," Dr. Hastings said and flipped through more of the papers, eventually he stopped and drew one from the pack. He turned it so that Paul could see it clearly on the desk.

There, scribbled in a trembling hand, was an image that Paul had tried very hard to forget. A dark figure covered the page, all the way to the edges. It had the figure of a man but was covered in a thick mat of blackish-brown fur. It was a simple drawing—like one created by a child's hand—but there were enough details to make out what the creature looked like. And one feature, in particular, was disturbingly accurate: its golden eyes searching for Paul's own from the page.

He wanted to shiver, to shake, to snatch the paper up and crumple it into a ball and throw it across the office. But he did none of those things. Instead, he simply shook his head at Dr. Hastings, holding his gaze.

"Just a fevered vision of a sick man, doctor," Paul said. "Perhaps my illness affected the part of my brain which had seen something like this long ago. Some mishmash of a creature from childhood nightmares." And yet, Paul remembered its smell. Gamey and strong. He remembered the feel of its fur under his hands, surprisingly soft. And he remembered those eyes...

The doctor was silent a moment. Then, "Perhaps," said Dr. Hastings slowly. He slid four more drawings similar to the first across the desk. "And yet. I ask you to look more closely, Paul. Are you certain that your belief is truly gone? Or is it instead that you want to tell your doctor what he wants to hear?"

Paul forced himself to study each of the pictures. He saw the creature, the Bigfoot, hunched near a small grove of bushes; another where he was mid-stride, his great, shaggy head turned toward Paul, its big arms hanging loosely by its sides, fingers nearly touching its knees, and then two more pages covered in drawings of the beast's face and those strange eyes like gold coins gleaming from its face. Paul looked at the drawings and kept his face expressionless. He'd learned in his work at the newspaper to create a blank slate of his features. Any expression when he was interviewing a source could lead their account in another direction. He'd trained himself to keep his face empty of emotion, keep himself neutral.

"They aren't very good," Paul said finally with a half-smile, and Dr. Hastings chuckled as he gathered them back into a pile.

"Never mind that. They were real. Well, real to you anyway, in that moment." Dr. Hastings leaned his arms on his desk and made a teepee with his fingers. He placed his chin directly in the center. "Paul, you've made good progress here. I'd like to see you gain your strength more fully and put on a little more weight. You're still sleeping well you say?"

"Yes, sir," Paul lied. "I am."

"Well, that is good. That is good. Sleep is restorative to the body and all of its systems. Never skimp on sleep, Paul." He wagged a paternal finger toward Paul's face. Paul clenched his teeth and forced his head to nod in agreement.

"Of course, sir."

"I see no reason, young man, why you shouldn't be back home for the New Year." Dr. Hastings smiled and began to gather his papers together.

"The New Year?" Paul spluttered. "But that's two months away! Surely I could be discharged before then?"

With the overcrowding, Paul was surprised that his release hadn't already been planned. But then, his family was paying privately. At five dollars a week, Dr. Hastings had little incentive to see him leave.

Perhaps he'd played his cards all wrong, Paul thought, anger jabbing into his chest. Rather than pretending to be fully healed, he should have been a troublesome patient. One who caused ruckuses and stirred up the other inmates. Then the good doctor might be more willing to let him go.

"No. No, Paul, I believe this is in your best interest," Dr. Hastings said. "Your very best interest. I will talk with the head of the workroom, young man, and let you know what I discover. I tend to believe, however, that you will be better utilized in the laundry at present. But we shall see. We shall see."

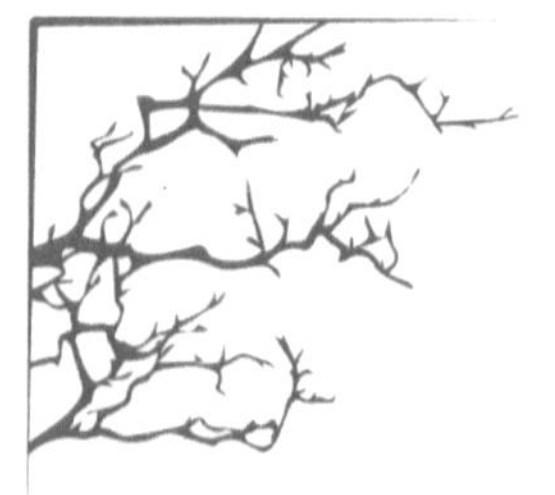

# Chapter Two

*Jane Rogers*
*Friday, September 7, 1917*
*Start of Shiny Creek Trail*

THEY'D BEEN WALKING only twenty minutes and already Jane could feel the city sliding off of her. It wasn't an unwelcome feeling. She enjoyed living in the city—restaurants, the theater, book readings, and other events—it was what she'd become used to. In the city, something was always happening. Out here though...Jane paused, watching her husband's back as he rounded a bend in the trail ahead of her. Out here there was only quiet. It was peaceful, but also unnerving. The constant sound of wheels, machinery clanking, people talking, and the hum of life was missing. The noises made up the background of Jane's days. She'd grown used to them.

The air here was different too: thick with the scent of pine needles and the earthy, sweet smell of decaying leaves underfoot. Above, tree branches danced in golden light, lit like candles by the sun. The leaves had just started to change. Green had turned to shades of yellow. Red and orange would come later in the season. For the most part, though, the forest looked like it did during the other times they'd hiked in summer.

Except, Jane couldn't shake the feeling that someone was watching them. She glanced over her shoulder for the tenth time and quickened her pace.

Silly.

Of course, she felt unnerved. The setting was completely at odds with normal daily life in Burlington. Why wouldn't she feel peculiar?

"Everything all right?" Paul asked. He'd stopped on the trail and Jane lost in thought, had nearly bumped into him.

"Yes, sorry," she said, her breath already coming a little harder in her chest. "Just thinking how beautiful it is here."

"It is that, isn't it?" Paul smiled as he tilted his head upward, taking in the leaves and branches and sunlight that formed the canopy above them. He turned back to her.

"Jane, I meant to ask you if this trip was really something you wanted to do." Paul returned his gaze to her, his eyes searching her face. "I mean, Allan and Deidre can be persuasive, you know that. But if you were uncomfortable, we could have bowed out. I suppose it's a little late to tell you this now, but—"

"I wouldn't have missed it," Janes said, forcing her tone to be cheerful. "Go, Paul, or we'll fall far behind the others."

Paul nodded. "If you're sure."

"Yes. Yes, I'm very sure."

He smiled at her and stuck his hands under his pack's straps to alleviate some of the pressure. He started walking again. Jane followed but her eyes smarted. Why did Paul automatically assume Jane would be uninterested or unwilling to go on an adventure like this? It was true she wasn't the most fearless in their little foursome, but she was hardly a wilting violet.

The two couples had been friends for so long that she sometimes forgot that originally it had been Deidre, Allan, and Paul—the Three Musketeers—who'd met in college. Paul's comment unintentionally hurt. It reminded Jane again that she was the outsider. Paul and their friends were photojournalists, while Jane was a mere secretary. She was the only one in the group who had grown up in the country, too, not Burlington where Paul was from, or Boston where Allan and Deidre were originally from.

What Paul said was true though: Deidre and Allan were always trying new things, going on new adventures. Jane wondered meanly sometimes if it wasn't only so that they could recount their harrowing tales to everyone.

Jane took a big breath and drew her shoulders back. Already an ache had formed between them from the heavy pack. While her work wasn't as exciting as the others, it was steady and reliable. Indeed, she's surprised her parents and Paul's by bringing her own savings account to their marriage, something that was unheard of a generation ago.

Paul had big dreams. His work at the newspaper was solid and steady but what he really wanted was to become a photojournalist for a big-name magazine like *National Geographic*. And why shouldn't he? Allan told him constantly that he could do it if only he'd set his mind to it. But there was something in Paul, some unnamed fear that Jane had come to recognize was pulling him back from his dream.

That's why this trip was so important. Shiny Creek Trail, deep in the Green Mountains of Vermont, was where eighteen-year-old James Smithfield had gone missing in 1897. It was also the location where several other people had been lost—some returned, some not—and the spot where a decade ago, three hunters had spotted the man-beast.

Jane shivered. The image in the newspaper that she'd found was still fresh in her mind. The monster, the Bigfoot—tall and shaggy—had filled her dreams for the past weeks since she'd found the article. But was it real? Or had the men taken a photograph of a friend dressed in a costume? It wasn't unheard of, the pranks people devised to gain publicity and capitalize on it.

Her foot caught on a root and she let out a small grunt before catching herself on a nearby sapling. Hunched over, she felt it again.

That feeling that someone's eyes were on her. She righted herself slowly, straightening her pack on her shoulders. Jane looked around. All along the path were trees, trees, and more trees. Bushes and other low-lying shrubs clambered over the forest floor, half-dead ferns and tilted stumps filled in otherwise bare areas.

Jane turned to the right and then to the left. But there was nothing out of the ordinary. No one out there: no heads peeking around tree trunks or faces camouflaged in the shrubbery. Still, she couldn't deny the feeling. She smoothed her hands over her front. She felt naked hiking in only bloomers. Perhaps it was simply that discomfort that made her feel conspicuous. Deidre seemed to enjoy it and had laughed gleefully as she'd tossed her skirt back into Allan's shiny new Peerless.

"Now we'll be as free as the birds," she'd said to Jane with a grin. Jane, always practical, had folded her skirt neatly and deposited it into her knapsack. If they met another group on the trail, she wanted to be ready to put it back on at a moment's notice. Paul, anticipating her discomfort, had told Deidre and Allan to start without them, that they'd be along momentarily. They would eventually see Jane in just the bloomers of course, but something was mortifying about removing her skirt in front of the others. She'd felt a wave of love toward Paul at his suggestion the others go on ahead. He was like that: always considerate, always thinking of her feelings.

Jane readjusted the bloomers' waistband and hitched her pack up higher. She tried to shake off the feeling of being watched and quickened her pace to catch up to Paul.

"DARLING, DON'T YOU want to snap a picture of me?" Deidre's voice, teasing, called to Allan across the campsite. Jane paused in hammering the tent peg to glance at her friend. Deidre, in true form, had applied a fresh coat of lipstick and plucked a handful of ferns that she used as a feather fan behind her head. With her auburn hair loose around her face and her body twisted into a sultry pose, she looked like a pinup girl in one of the magazines Jane's boss hid in his bottom desk drawer.

Jane shook her head, smiling, as she went back to pounding the peg. It had gone in easily at first but now vibrated in her hand under the mallet. Paul squatted beside her and grinned. He smelled good: pine and the faint trace of aftershave mixed with sweat.

"You might have hit a rock," he said. "Want me to give it a crack?"

"Yes, please," Jane said gratefully. She stood. Her legs and back ached a bit. She felt tired but exhilarated. They'd hiked deep into the forest, at least six miles from the pull-off where they'd left Allan's car. The ascent hadn't been overly steep—not yet—but Deidre had looked grateful when Paul had suggested they stop and make camp in the late afternoon. Allan, in contrast, had been disappointed. Jane could tell by the tight line of his mouth, but he hadn't said anything. As for herself, Jane could have kept going for at least another hour or two. Her body was tired but not fatigued.

She'd always had great stamina. "My little mule," her mother had often referred to Jane as growing up. Not the most flattering comparison, but it was true. In Jane's family, being strong and able to weather storms was a given, so "mule" in her mother's mind had likely been a fine compliment.

"Mule?" Paul had said incredulously when she'd told him once. "No. No, that's not right at all." He'd frowned. "There are many other "m" words to describe you. Marvelous, minx, magnanimous, miraculous—"

"Stop!" Jane had laughed then as Paul had pulled her over on top of him on the picnic blanket. He'd tickled her face with his scratchy jaw, then pulled back and looked at her, the laughter faded from his eyes.

"And the most important m-word of all." He'd said and his voice had grown deeper.

"What's that?" Jane had asked. Her hands on his chest, she'd propped herself up to look at him more easily.

"Mine."

She'd felt a thrill as his lips had covered hers gently at first, then more urgently. His hands had caressed her arms gently, then moved to her sides. Then they were traveling over her entire body until she was warm and breathless, her skin pink, her eyes closed. Waiting for—

"...did you, Jane?"

Jane opened her eyes, her cheeks hot with embarrassment.

"Pardon?"

"I just asked if you'd brought any of the articles along with you, other than the two we'd talked about this morning," Deidre said, walking over. She'd discarded her ferns and was pinning the front of her hair up out of her face. She'd knotted her shirt up in the front, showing a pale swath of flat belly between her blouse and bloomers.

"Oh, no, I'm sorry," Jane said. "I brought just the article about James Smithfield and the one about the hunters."

"Oh, don't give it another thought," Deidre said, waving a hand through the air. "I just wondered, that's all. My, your tent looks inviting," she said, peering at the perfectly taut sides of the Rogers' tent. "Would you like to switch?" Deidre cast a disparaging look at the tent Allan was still erecting. It hung droopily from the poles, its sides wrinkled.

"I'm sure he'll have it looking just as good in no time," Jane said, brushing her hands together. "I was going to start a fire. Would you like to help me gather wood?"

"Oh," Deidre said, wrinkling her nose. "I suppose so."

"Did you have something else you wanted to do instead?" Jane asked.

"No, not really. Well, to be honest, put my feet up and read a book but I suppose that would be bad form considering my husband is sweating and swearing at the moment."

As if on cue, Allan muttered something under his breath, the cigarette in his lips wobbling.

Deidre grinned at Jane. "Yes, let's go collect sticks, shall we?"

"I'll put on a pot of coffee when we get back," Jane promised.

"And I'll pull out the whiskey for a little extra boost," Deidre said.

Jane laughed. The women linked arms and headed into the woods.

It took no time at all to find enough dry branches to build a roaring fire. They were about to head back to camp when Jane paused. Deidre was a few feet away. She'd abandoned her pile of sticks and was picking wide leaves from a plant that she wove into a crown.

"It's for Allan," Deidre said in a conspiratorial whisper. "King of the tentmakers." She laughed. Jane smiled. She was about to look away when something moved behind Deidre. A few tree branches nearby shook and then were still. The wind? But there wasn't any, not even a slight breeze. Deidre caught Jane's eye.

"What is it?" she asked, her hands growing still.

Jane motioned for her to be quiet, her eyes still searching the branches near her friend. There was nothing though, no movement, no sound.

Everything was still.

Jane let out her breath and smiled.

Then the leaves nearest Deidre moved again. Deidre whirled around. The leaf crown flew from her hands. She stumbled backward, toward Jane who met Deidre halfway and pulled her back. Faster, faster from the thing that was rattling the branches and shaking the leaves.

Was it a bobcat? A bear? Jane searched her memory for predatory wild animals in the state. Panthers. Did they still have panthers here or had they all been hunted out? She searched the trees and low-growing shrubs nearby, looking for any movement. For the flash of tan or brown fur. She expected any minute to see a large, furry body hurl itself toward them, roaring. But there was nothing.

"Maybe just a raccoon or some other animal walking past," she whispered finally to Deidre. "We should get back to camp though. Can you manage your branches? If not, I can—"

"Look!" Deidre's voice hissed hot against her ear. "Something is there." She pointed her finger shaking.

Jane felt an icy trickle of fear fall down her backbone. She looked. Where Deidre had been standing moments before, the branches were settled back into place. Nothing was amiss. Jane saw only the same dull, tired leaves of autumn and the tangled undergrowth. She was about to turn to her friend and ask what she meant.

Then she saw it.

In a crack between two large trees, hidden was a dark shape. More shadow than hard lines. A man? But no. Much too large. It was hunched over, as though looking for something on the ground.

"Bear," Deidre's whisper was barely audible. "What do we do?"

Jane shook her head. Everything felt slowed down, the air molasses-thick. The animal raised itself slightly higher. It was massively tall. Jane swallowed hard. Branches undulated around the animal's shape. It was hard to make out in the thick undergrowth.

Jane stood, mesmerized. In the dim light of the woods, the dark shadow against dark branches was nearly impossible to see. Then, for one instant, Jane saw its head in profile. Shaggy. Large—larger than any animal she'd ever seen. Huge, in fact. But there was something else. Something that her brain was trying to process but failing to. She realized suddenly what it was: the animal's profile was all wrong. Flat where its snout should have stuck out. Like a bear missing its nose or a panther standing upright—but neither of those images made any sense.

"Run!" Deidre hissed again. She grabbed Jane's hand and pulled her back toward the trail.

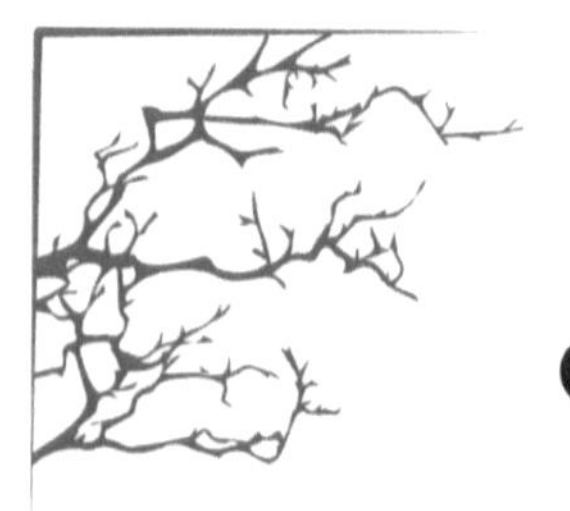

# Chapter Three



*Paul Rogers*
*Monday, November 5, 1917*
*Vermont State Hospital for the Insane*

HE MUST BE ABSOLUTELY crazy. Paul clenched his fists and forced himself to breathe. The silly girl in front of him—Martha, the young kitchen helper—was yammering on and on about her desire to be an author.

"...don't you think so?"

He smiled and gave her a wink. "I think you can do anything you set your mind to, Miss Shirley. Now, about that favor?"

Her face—open, smooth, and honest—grew shadows around the edges. "Oh, I'm just not sure. I don't think my fiancé would approve."

Paul felt his breath tighten, then stop in his chest. This had to work. It had to. He couldn't wait until January for his release. Jane could still be alive out there. Wandering around, cold and afraid. Hungry. He'd left her to fend for herself. His wife, his love. His Jane.

Paul dug deep and plastered a big smile on his face. "Miss Shirley, do you know what makes one a good writer? What separates the average pack from the elite? What sets apart your..." He searched his mind frantically for the name of the British mystery author Martha loved. "May Edginton from the rest?"

She shook her head slowly.

"It's courage, Miss Shirley. Courage that these writers experienced in their real life and which later shows up on the page. Now, you could argue that breaking a rule here or there isn't courageous. You might even think it foolish. But I ask you, Miss Shirley, what adventure hasn't included a few broken rules? Did Lewis and Clark follow the rules perfectly to explore new territories? Did President Washington follow the rules of war when he attacked the Hessians on Christmas Day?"

Martha's face was rapt, her eyes focused completely on Paul.

Let this work. It *must* work.

"There can be no fulfillment of dreams if there is no courage, Miss Shirley," Paul said. His voice trembled slightly. Martha no doubt believed it to be from conviction. Truthfully, it was desperation.

"Yes," Martha said, her voice less timid. "Yes, I see your point." She took a deep breath and let it out, her shoulders straightening as she did so. Paul could almost see the gears spinning in her mind as she debated with her conscience.

"All right then. I will help you. I'll tell Jacques that it is for love. That, he will understand." Her cheeks bloomed pink and Paul wanted to rush forward and grab the girl in his arms, leap about the room with her crowing.

Instead, he smiled in what he hoped was a benign manner. "You'll make a fine author someday," he said. "Of that, I have no doubt."

HIS ESCAPE WAS ARRANGED for that Wednesday. The truck from the Brattleboro furniture shop arrived at the asylum at nine o'clock. Then the driver—a silly-looking old codger with a wild beard and nearly bald head—would go directly to the kitchen for breakfast. He was completely smitten with one of the cooks, Martha had told Paul and would dally as long as possible over his meal. Jacques usually waited until the driver returned to load up the truck with the new chairs and other small wooden furniture that had been produced. This time though, Martha had convinced her fiancé to get the furniture on straightaway, allowing Paul a precious minute to stow away in the deepest, darkest spot in the truck and hide there.

Paul had no money at the asylum. He had, however, promised Martha that when he returned home, he'd send her five dollars. "A nuptial gift for you and Jacques," he'd said with a wink. Martha had blushed red and thanked him. The two planned to elope later that month, a secret that Martha had confided when Paul told her of his desire to get out of the asylum and back to his wife.

Now, Paul stood at the corner of the building in the shadows. He'd crept out of the hallway when the aide's back was turned, a surprisingly easy feat in the steamy bowels of the asylum's laundry rooms. He'd begun working in the massive laundry room three days ago, quickly learning the job and all it entailed. It was hard, hot work that left his mind lots and lots of time to roam. He'd used it to plan out every step of his escape and the journey beyond. Because of his current mental stability—along with the unknown talent of regurgitating his pills—Paul was given more freedom within the building by Dr. Hastings. In fact, the good doctor had himself introduced Paul to Mr. Connolly, the head of the laundry. "You're doing well, Paul. Doing well," Dr. Hastings had said with a half-hearted slap on the back.

The smell of soap and bleach still filled his nose now as Paul watched the furniture truck intently. He saw a young, slim man emerge from the building. He was dressed in work clothes, with a woolen cap jauntily set on his dark, curled hair. This was Jacques, Martha's fiancé, a transplant from Quebec.

Jacques greeted the driver whose bushy beard stuck out a foot from his face and covered his chest and belly. The spindly man waved his arm toward the building as he talked to Jacques. The Frenchman shook his head in response, then listened another moment and nodded before re-plying.

What was happening? Was this a normal conversation or was Jacques telling the driver of his fiancée's plan to help a crazy man? Paul's fingernails dug into his damp palms. A single word spun around in his head in short, jerky circles: Jane.

Jane. Jane. Jane. Jane. Jane.

Then, finally, the bearded man nodded and ambled off toward the door of the building. Minutes later, Jacques gave a short, low whistle. That was the signal. Paul crouched and ran to the side of the truck fur-thest from the building.

"You go here," a voice said in Paul's ear. He hadn't even heard the younger man approach. "Stay down. No see, eh? No see you." Paul climbed up the side of the tarp-covered truck and burrowed into the corner. An old horse blanket that smelled of mildew and something even worse was lying in a heap nearby. He quickly swept it over him, making himself as small as possible.

"Remember, eh?" Jacques spoke from the side of the truck, tighten-ing the ropes. "No noise. You make go before truck stop."

Paul nodded, then realized Jacques couldn't see him through the truck's tarp. "Yes. I will."

It seemed hours before Jacques finished loading the chairs and small tables into the truck and longer still until the driver re-emerged from the building, smelling of bacon grease and coffee. Paul's stomach grumbled. He'd had nothing to eat since last night's dinner.

The men talked briefly.

"What, you loaded it all up did you?"

"Ah, yes. Simple today. Easy go."

"Well, thank you. Thank you kindly. You have yourself a good week now."

"*Oui*. You do same."

And they were off. The truck rumbled to life and Paul bounced back and forth like a tennis ball between the pieces of furniture closest to him before the truck pulled onto the main road. Then the ride smoothed with only an occasional jostle or teeth-snapping bounce.

Paul stretched his legs out and threw the blanket to the side. Before it hit the floor of the truck he saw a gray knapsack. It was the type used by the asylum when inmates had day trips. Each was labeled clearly with a label that shouted, "Vermont State Hospital for the Insane." He pulled it toward him eagerly and opened it. At the top was a piece of paper folded in two. Opening it, Paul saw the neat, curly script of a woman's hand.

*For Romeo as he seeks his Juliet. Nourishment for the journey. May true love always win!*
*Yours in admiration,*
*Miss Martha Shirley*

Paul's smile broadened as he dug into the pack. Inside was a canteen full of water, a dented flashlight, a small, empty pot, matches, a loaf of bread, a chunk of cheese, three apples, and another, smaller bag filled with ginger cookies. God bless Martha Shirley.

IT TOOK PAUL NEARLY two days to reach the small town of Glaston. It was just outside of the tiny town that Shiny Creek Trail began. The town featured two rows of tidy but plain houses, one church, a general store that boasted both an apothecary and post office inside and a small bakery. He could smell the leftover scent of cinnamon and warm bread in the air as he passed behind the building.

The night had been growing dark when he arrived. Paul had been let out by one of the many motorists he'd gotten rides from since jumping from the furniture truck outside of Brattleboro. The leap into the undergrowth had hurt. His leg, which always ached, had felt fiery that night as he'd sat by the small fire in the woods. Paul worried that he'd done serious damage, but the next morning after he'd walked off the stiffness in his limbs, it hadn't felt any worse than usual.

Now, he passed by the last of the small houses. Dinner smells edged out from under the doorframe and around the windows. The smell of something meaty and warm made his mouth fill with saliva. Hunger had plagued him since leaving the asylum. His belly pinched and grumbled but he rationed the food in small allotments. If he found Jane—no when he found Jane—he wanted to give the food to her. She'd be so hungry.

An image came to mind, one he continually tried to block out but that crept in anyway. Jane, half-naked in the chill November air, dirty and bedraggled. Jane, bruised, with cuts and scrapes bleeding. Her former luscious curves and sturdy planes replaced with protruding bones and sagging skin. Jane, with haunted eyes filled with fear...

Paul shook his head, trying to clear it. As though the thoughts were a spider's web that could be torn down. Jane was resourceful and strong. She was still alive, still intact. She'd have sought solace in the forest. Solace from that thing...

Other images came then.

No.

He couldn't indulge himself in regret over what had happened. Not now. All his energy, his focus had to go into getting to the trail and finding Jane. Shivering—whether from fear or the cold, he wasn't sure—Paul crept alongside the last house in front of him. This one stood off a ways from the others on the street. From the slightly neglected look of it, Paul guessed it had been the first one built. He took a chance and peeked into a window. A family was just preparing for dinner. Two little girls set the table and a tiny boy, crying, clung to his mother's skirt as she stood at the stove. Paul edged away from the window. More smells of cooking food emanated from the little house and flowed by him in the cold night air. His stomach growled.

He moved stealthily toward the small chicken coop. Stealing one of the birds was tempting but too much of a risk. Chickens tended to squawk and make other loud noises. Instead, Paul had decided to go after the eggs.

Propping open the door of the coop, he was hit with the ammonia smell of chicken droppings and the more pleasant scent of hay. He couldn't see anything in the dim room but felt his way around the corners and shapes. First, a pitchfork that he nearly knocked over, then a barrel. He found the first nesting box and scrabbled around it with his hands. It was empty, save for the hay. He made his way around the tiny room, feeling first in one box and then another. A few had chickens in them, but most sat along the top, roosting for the night. They were quiet, other than an occasional murmur when he thumped one with his hand.

Finally, the fifth and seventh boxes had what he was looking for. Paul scooped the three eggs into his pockets and retraced his steps in the dark, finding his way out of the coop. From there, he made his way to the dirt road that led further into the woods. He walked for a long time, trying to pick out landmarks from when they'd driven through here in Allan's big Peerless. He recognized the covered bridge but little else in the dim light. About twenty minutes later, Paul found the grassy pull-off across from Shiny Creek Trail. Paul had been half-worried that he wouldn't be able to find it again. He could see the spot where they'd left Allan's car that day, and when he closed his eyes momentarily, he could hear the voices of Jane and his friends as they'd called to each other, excitedly loading packs onto their backs.

Now, Paul gently laid his own smaller pack down. The air was brisk and the moon was half full, helping him to get his bearings as he gathered sticks. After he'd gotten a small pile, he moved to the edge of the clearing with a clear line to the road and squatted to start layering the sticks and branches. Tonight, he'd dine like a king.

Later, after the fire had died down and Paul had wrapped himself and his knapsack up with the horse blanket, he again went over his next steps. He'd been able to refill the canteen and take a long, satisfying drink from a well in town. That would keep him at least a couple of days if he were careful with it. It would be a two-day hike at least to the cave.

The cave.

More images flooded into Paul's mind at the word. Dark, dank walls. The smell of mustiness and earthy decomposition. The light bouncing from their nickel-plated flashlights on the cave walls. And then, later...

He'd need to get an early start, Paul reminded himself and turned on his side. He drew his knapsack tight to his belly. He shouldn't keep it with him. It could attract any bears who weren't yet in hibernation or other animals to him. But he was too tired to try to hang it from a nearby tree. And anyway, he didn't have any rope. He'd hoped to find some—a laundry line in town—but hadn't had any success.

It would be all right. He was only going to sleep for a couple of hours. He wanted to get an early start.

He was just drifting off, the firm tug of sleep pulling him under when he heard it. A small cry—a mewl really—that snapped his eyes open.

His thoughts instantly went to Jane. He pushed the blanket away and let the knapsack tumble to the ground.

"Jane?" he whispered loudly. "Jane, is that you?"

There was silence for a moment. Then a single branch snapped loudly across the clearing. It sounded like a gunshot in the quiet meadow. Paul swung his head wildly in that direction. His heartbeat crashed in his eardrums. Without moving his eyes from the tree line where the noise had come from, Paul scrabbled a hand over his pack, searching for his flashlight.

He needn't have bothered. At that moment, Paul's eyes connected with the light eyes staring back at him. Paul stared dumbly at the animal. Its fur was golden and even in the dim light of the quarter moon, Paul could see the sharp, yellowed teeth of the catamount. They were latched around the body of a limp rabbit. The small gray creature's head hung loose. Its dead eyes stared as though looking directly at Paul with a warning.

Go back.

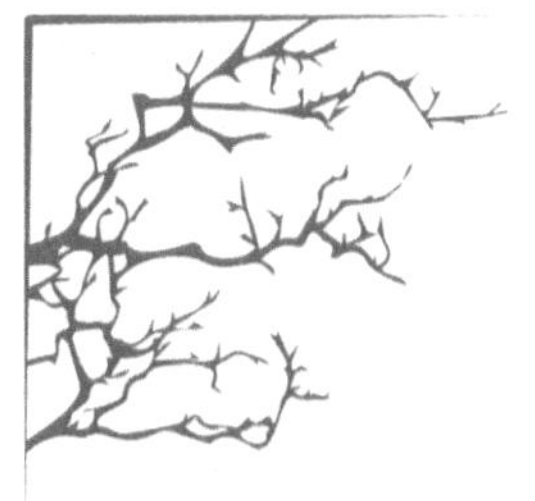

# Chapter Four

*Jane Rogers*
*Saturday, September 8, 1917*
*Shiny Creek Trail*

IT WAS LATE AFTERNOON the next day. Jane's legs ached and her back felt permanently bent in a slight "c" position. But it was beautiful in the woods. Everywhere Jane looked there was greenness in various shades: gentle shades on the feathery ferns, stronger shades on the prickly bushes and tall grasses, and the bright, almost fluorescent green of the moss growing on the boulders they passed. Soft sunlight had lit their way most of the morning. But thick gray clouds had shouldered their way in when the group had stopped for lunch. Now, the atmosphere felt thick and weighted, as though the clouds were pressing down on them with great, heavy hands.

"I don't like the look of those."

Jane, propped against a tree and covered a yawn then looked up at the sky, following Paul's gaze. He was right. The clouds were growing darker in the little patch of sky visible between the treetops.

Allan groaned. "Not rain, too."

"Afraid so," Paul said. "But I think we've got an hour or so at least to make camp."

"But that'll put us off track timewise. You know we've got at least a few more hours hike to get to the spot where young James went missing."

"I know it. And I also know that we're not going to be able to make it there before this weather hits. Look," Paul turned his head to look at their little group. "It's not my decision. What do you bunch think?"

"I say we press on," Allan said immediately.

Deidre moaned in response to that idea. "I have blisters the size of Montana. Darling, let's build camp for the night here and start fresh tomorrow morning. Besides, none of us slept more than a wink last night."

Jane held back a shiver. Deidre had been hysterical enough for the both of them last night when they'd fled back to the others without their branches.

"There's a bear. A bear, Allan!" she'd yelled, running into camp, her hair flying behind her. Doubled over and gasping for air, the women had finally related what they'd seen in the forest. It wasn't much.

"A large, brown animal...might have been a bear," Jane said, getting her breath back first.

"No, it was black," Deidre insisted. "Huge."

"How huge?" Allan asked, holding his wife's arms with his hands. Jane could see the diamond-encrusted wedding band he wore indenting Deidre's skin slightly.

"Huge."

"Jane?" Allan had turned to her, releasing Deidre's arms. "Was it a bear?"

"I...I'm not sure. I think so. Probably yes."

"Which way was it headed?" Paul asked.

Jane shook her head. "I'm not sure it was headed anywhere. It...it was just standing there when we saw it."

"Did it look hungry?" This question came from Allan and for some reason struck Deidre as funny. She started to laugh, then covered her mouth, her eyes beginning to tear up. Jane too, couldn't help letting a laugh out and finally, Paul and Allan joined in. There was a touch of hysteria to the laughter though. Jane guessed it was a natural response to the fear they were feeling. After all, what weapons did they have out here if a bear or other animal attacked? The cameras were solid and could do some damage if swung hard enough, she supposed. But hoped to God they didn't have to get close enough to any bear to find out.

*Or any other animal.* The thought crept into her brain and stuck there. She should tell them what she thought she'd seen. It's why they were here, after all, wasn't it? To find out the mystery that made up these woods. If what she'd seen was real—if it was a man-beast, a Bigfoot—the group had a right to know. But had she really seen it or had her eyes been tricking her? She closed them momentarily. Tried to remember exactly what she'd seen when she'd peered through the dark foliage at the dark animal that had been hidden in shadow. Had it been real? Didn't the others have a right to know, even if she only suspected it?

And yet...

Jane couldn't force the words out. Because already she didn't quite fit in with the rest of the group. And if she was the one saying she'd seen a beast—a monster—while Deidre had seen only a bear...

Jane shook her head now and said, "I think it would be best to look for a place to make camp for the night—"

Allan groaned. "Of course, you'd say that. He's your husband."

"But—I wasn't finished—why can't we wait as long as possible to do so? It's not as though there's a spot right here flat enough to set up the tents." She motioned to the steep section of the trail where they were resting. "The map shows that there are some caves a little further up. Maybe we could take shelter there and wait out the storm. Then get a fresh start in the morning like Deidre said."

Deidre smiled at her gratefully. "That's a wonderful idea, cookie."

Allan frowned. "Where about are these caves?"

"I'm not sure. Paul, can we see the map?"

He was one step ahead of her though, already unfolding it and spreading it on a nearby log.

They studied it. Or rather, Paul, Jane, and Allan did. Deidre closed her eyes. "I'm hopeless at maps," she said. "Just wake me up when you want me to start walking again."

Allan rolled his eyes but smiled slightly at least. "Shouldn't take too long, maybe twenty minutes?"

Paul shook his head. "Three-quarters of an hour at least I'd wager. The trail is getting steeper—" This brought a groan from Deidre.

"And look how little ground we've covered this morning compared to yesterday."

Allan nodded. "Yes, well. If we'd gotten better sleep we'd have more capacity today." His voice was still tinged with annoyance.

"Let's go," Jane said. "The sooner we find the cave the sooner we can relax, take our packs off and sit down."

"Sounds good to me," Paul said and offered her a brief smile. It didn't quite reach his eyes though and Jane knew why. He was worried. They all were. Sure, there had been no signs of a bear or other predatory animal today. But that didn't mean it wasn't out there, just that they weren't observant enough or had missed the signs. Some animals, like mountain cats, were so stealthy one didn't know they were nearby until it was too late.

They gathered their packs and reformed a line. This time Jane led with the map in her hand. Paul bent his head close to hers so the others couldn't hear. "I'll keep an eye out. Don't worry."

She smiled then, but couldn't stop the hair from rising along the back of her neck.

They soon fell into a familiar rhythm. *Step, step, step, step.* Swipe a hand over one's forehead or upper lip or adjust a pack strap. *Step, step, step, step.* Jane listened for any sounds out of the ordinary. But for four people, they made an incredible amount of noise. Their boots over the fallen dry leaves sounded like waves washing up on the beach but constant and louder. She looked around every few feet, eyeing the trees and brush warily.

The night before, Paul and Jane had retraced the women's steps. Allan had wanted to go too, but Deidre had clung to him. "No, please don't leave me here alone."

It hadn't been hard to find the route they'd taken. Broken branches and an occasional muddy footprint led them to the spot where piles of branches were scattered on the ground. Jane and Paul had moved around in a widening circle, looking for signs of any kind of animal. But they'd seen nothing. In the end, they'd gathered up the sticks and branches and had gone back to camp.

Allan was right: none of them had slept well. Every creak and crack and hoot and far-away howl had jerked them from a fitful slumber. They'd risen early, eaten a hasty breakfast, and packed up quickly.

Thunder rolled across the dark sky to the far right of them now. Jane shivered and checked the map again. It shouldn't be much further.

IN THE END, THE STORM passed them by. The thunder had continued rumbling in the distance but then moved further and further away until finally, it rolled out of the region. Jane breathed a sigh of relief. Everyone was tired and sore and hungry. She was grateful they wouldn't have to add the discomfort of wet blankets, packs, and feet to the experience.

"Should we stay or press on?" Jane asked. Now that the threat of a storm had passed, they'd make it to their destination, a little camping area further along Shiny Creek Trail near a brook. It was here that James Smithfield had intended to go. It might have been the last place he'd camped before disappearing.

The little group stood now outside the cave from the map. It was positioned a significant distance from the path and was larger than Jane had expected. A cursory glance inside told them it was dry and animal-free. There were still hours of daylight left, and Allan wanted to keep going. He'd been talking about it since they'd headed toward the cave.

"This isn't a pleasure trip," he'd grumbled when Deidre had asked if they couldn't just slow down a little. "We're here to find answers. To write a story, Dee. That's hard to do if we aren't at the actual location of the event."

"And you know how important that is to me too, darling. But we're behind the eight ball here. Let's take a rest and reassess."

So, they'd gone off the path and found the cave. Jane shivered now as she looked at it. Why? It promised a warm, dry place to sleep. But that feeling was back. That someone was watching her, watching them. The cave itself looked sinister, like a hulking gargoyle perched on the side of the mountain's side.

"Jane?" Allan swung his gaze to her. "Once again, you're the only one who hasn't spoken up."

"Lay off, Allan." Paul's voice was quiet but his eyes had a hard look to them.

Jane put a hand on her husband's arm. "I've just been thinking, that's all," she said. "Truthfully, I could go on. I feel strong enough. But Deidre needs rest and the thought of a dry spot for the night, out of the wind—" a strong wind had picked up, the fallout from the storm that had passed by— "doesn't sound unappealing to me. So, I vote that we stay."

Allan sighed and threw up his hands. "Outvoted again."

Deidre smiled up at him and gave a wink. "Oh, cookie. It's just a few hours. We'll get an even earlier start in the morning, we'll be so fresh and new feeling."

Allan didn't smile. Instead, he stalked into the cave and gently lowered his heavy pack with one of the cameras in it to the ground.

"I'm going to take a look around," he told them over his shoulder and moved off into the cave.

"He's just sulking," Deidre said and groaned as she stood up again from the large rock she'd been sitting on. "He'll get over it soon."

But he didn't.

That night as they sat around the campfire at the entrance of the cave, Allan's mood was worse than before. He hit his shin on a rock while retrieving more branches from the pile and cursed, then swore at Deidre when she accidentally bumped it later on.

Everyone's mood deteriorated in the cave. Jane wasn't one to assign feelings to inanimate objects, but if she was, she'd say that this place wasn't filled with happy, glad tidings. It was cold and dank of course—it was a cave after all—but there was something else. A sort of pressing, dark feeling. Like the air itself was heavier and weighed them all down. It didn't help that the wind screamed around the entrance to the cave, moaning and shrieking like a banshee from a scary children's story.

Had the cave been the right choice? Jane glanced around. The firelight played on the walls, making shadows dance. It was warm and dry. They'd eaten a hot meal cooked over the fire and sipped a little of Deidre's whiskey laced with coffee. They had room to set out all their things—their bedrolls, their makeshift pillows. It should have felt cozy and safe. Instead, an ominous feeling clung to Jane like a foul smell.

She was being ridiculous. "Silly little sailor," her father would have called her. She laid her head against Paul's shoulder. It felt solid and warm.

"Sleepy?" he asked and dropped a kiss onto her forehead.

She shook her head but yawned.

He chuckled.

"Well. Maybe just a little," she said.

A branch in the fire popped and sparks shot upward. Jane followed them, her gaze lazily tracing the contours of the rock ceiling above. It was high, the dark gray stone washed in orangish light from the fire below.

What was that? Her head jerked from Paul's shoulder as she craned her neck to see more clearly. Painted along the roof of the cave directly over their fire, were strange markings. No, symbols. She recognized the eye first, wide and staring. Other marks looked like hieroglyphics or something similar that she couldn't make out. Her eyes widened as she took in the other image: penning them in was a large five-pointed star. A pentagram.

She pointed to it. "Did you see that?"

Paul looked up. She felt his arm stiffen beneath her own.

"What is it?" she asked.

He shook his head. "I don't know," he let out a breath that stirred her hair. "But it doesn't look very civilized, does it?"

Deidre had fallen asleep, curled in a blanket near the fire, her mouth partly open. Allan took another swig from his flask and frowned at Jane before following her pointing finger upward.

He swore under his breath and then got to his feet. Quickly, Allan stepped over his wife. Rummaging through his pack he extracted his camera. It was top of the line—of course, it was Allan's—and Jane wondered if he'd ever used it before.

"That's a great find, Jane," he'd said as though she'd gone looking for it. "I can't believe none of us saw it before now."

"It might be the angle we're sitting at," Jane said. "If you move back or forward a few inches, they seem to blend into the surface of the stone." The ceiling of the cave was high here and the symbols were drawn in black and a deep brownish-red, nearly blending in with the lumpy stone overhead.

Allan snapped several photos, muttering about the poor quality of the light until Jane shone a flashlight on the drawings. He gave her a quick smile.

"What do you think it means?" he asked later when he'd taken his seat again. He passed the flask to Paul who tipped it back and then handed it to Jane. She took a small sip and felt the whiskey burn along her esophagus and into her belly before giving it back.

"It looks old," Jane said. "Maybe Indians did it?"

"Maybe," Paul said. He was studying the ceiling again. "I don't like the look of that eye. Feels like it's watching us. And the pentagram isn't too reassuring either."

Allan snorted. "Old wives' tales," he said and got up to retrieve the flask from Paul. She felt Paul shift beside her.

"What did you find deeper in the cave, Allan?" Jane asked, trying to break the tension. "I hear running water."

Allan didn't answer at first, his eyes still hard and pinned on the fire in front of them. The flames were burning lower and Paul reached over and stirred the coals with a thick stick. Then he added another few branches. As if on cue, the wind screamed more loudly around the opening of the cave.

"There's a brook or underground creek or something way back. The cave is very long—much more so than you'd think from the outside. It must go deep underground. I didn't go all the way to the end, but if you go exploring, be careful. There's a ravine that drops off. The water source is at the bottom of it."

"We should fill our canteens," Jane said. "Then we'll be ready for an early start tomorrow."

"I'll do it," Paul said and rose to his feet. Jane immediately felt a shiver overtake her as the heat from his body vanished. "Give me your canteens, Allan, would you?"

Allan rummaged in their packs and found two brand-new, shiny canteens which he handed to Paul.

"Want company?" Jane asked and rose to her feet.

"No, you stay here by the fire." Paul reached down for one of the flashlights and hung the canteen straps around his neck. "I'll be back before you know it."

Jane felt a trickle of discomfort start along her neck. But why? She poked the fire and glanced at Allan. Did he feel it too? He was staring into the flames again.

"All right," she said to Paul. "Hurry back."

Paul's footsteps faded. Jane looked at Allan.

"I'll be outside for a moment," she said. "I need to use the, uh, facilities." She tilted her head to the forest beyond the cave's entrance. Allan seemed to rouse himself from a waking dream and looked at her. His eyes were bleary and slightly bloodshot.

"Sure. I'm going to turn in. I'm tired all of the sudden."

Jane nodded and took a flashlight. The wind outside the cave whipped the tree branches and leaves overhead. She put a hand out in front of her face, the beam of light bobbing and jerking over the uneven ground. The air had gotten colder but smelled fresh and delicious after the musty interior of the cave.

Finding a bush downhill, Jane relieved herself and then started to walk back to the cave. Something cracked overhead and she let out a yelp. She shone the flashlight beam up. A thick branch started to fall. Jane instinctively put an arm up over her head expecting to feel the heavy smack of wood against her arm. Instead, there was just the wind snagging her sleeve. She looked up again. The branch had caught on some others and tangled there. It swayed precariously though, and Jane quickly moved on.

Yellow light glittered in the distance. Had she gone that far from the cave? She turned, correcting her course and maneuvering around downed logs and tangles of ferns and dead vines. It wasn't until she was within ten feet that Jane realized the yellow light wasn't firelight at all.

And another sound beneath the wind filled her ears. The *huh-huh-huh* of panting nearby.

She stood motionless. The yellow light went out. She closed her own eyes. Her feet felt glued to the ground. Then her eyelids snapped open and she searched the forest around her. *Oh God, oh God.* Was it the bear?

Or that thing they'd seen earlier?

The creature. The Bigfoot.

*Huh-huh-huh.* The panting was getting louder, closer.

Branches snapped. Jane closed her eyes, trying to think.

What should she do? Run? Scream? Whirl around with a branch and shake it at the thing? A strange smell filled her nostrils. Gamey, strong.

When Jane was a little girl her uncle shot a deer once. "Venison for dinner, dear," her mother had said, trying to console Jane who'd burst into tears when she'd seen the dead buck's lifeless eyes and lolling tongue. The smell now was the same, only stronger and tinged with something else. Something earthier and more pungent.

*Huh-huh-huh.*

Closer.

Her eyes were wide now, her breath coming in quiet gasps.

Jane ran.

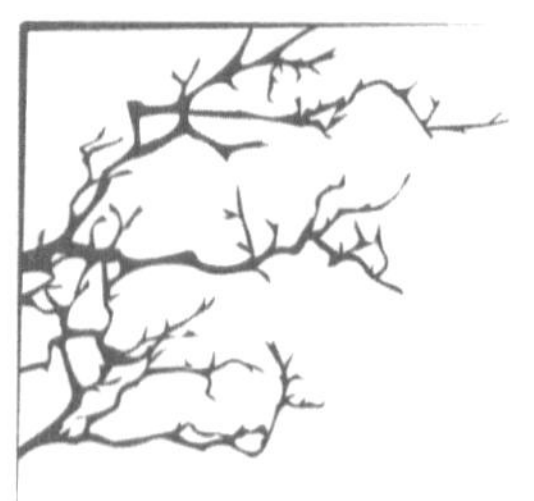

# Chapter Five



*Paul Rogers*
*Saturday, November 10, 1917*
*Shiny Creek Trail*

WHEN PAUL WAS GROWING up, hard work was a given. Cows had to be milked before dawn split the sky. Fences needed mending, buildings needed constant repair, and there was always—always—work to be done wherever one looked. He'd liked it when he was very young. Before he'd realized the monotony that came from trying and failing to ever get ahead. By adolescence he'd understood this truth: no matter how many tasks you completed, there were always ten, twenty, or thirty more lurking. Summers as a teenager had been spent wiping sweat out of his eyes and swearing to himself that he would not—not ever—follow in his father's and grandfather's footsteps.

The one thing that farming had been good for was letting his imagination bloom. Farm work was challenging physically but not mentally and he spent hours plowing or hoeing or digging or milking lost in the stories he created in his mind. When he'd left the farm at seventeen—the first one in his family to ever attend college—it hadn't been with a flurry of good wishes.

He'd had to drop out for a semester that first year and take on odd jobs. Then he'd worked, ironically, on a farm to earn enough to continue school. Whereas his peers completed their degrees in four years, it had taken Paul six. But he'd done it. Even his father had slapped his back extra hard on graduation day and offered a smile that stretched from ear to ear. His mother had wiped away tears, blaming her misty eyes on the pollen in the air.

Now, Paul's breath came hard in his chest. He'd lost his farm conditioning but was still making good time. Despite the cold, sweat trickled down the back of his neck. Jacques had snuck him an old coat under the tarp in the truck before the driver had emerged from the asylum that morning. Paul loosened the buttons now, letting the cold November air seep in.

He paused along the trail. It looked markedly different than when they'd been here just two months ago. In place of the bushy trees above, bare branches pointed like witches' fingers into the sky. The trail was harder to make out, covered in a carpet of thick, decomposing leaves. They made it slippery, too. More than once he'd caught himself on a nearby tree or bush when his feet slipped on the path. The air smelled of earth and the sweet fragrance of the dead leaves underfoot. His pack was lighter now than it had been in September too, but his feet felt heavier, along with his heart.

The image of Jane appeared again in his mind, but he shoved it back. He had to focus. Had to get back to the cave where everything had fallen apart. Where they had fallen apart...

Twigs snapped nearby. Paul whirled in that direction. He was sure he'd see the creature—huge and covered in fur—emerge from the woods. Paul raised the stick he'd been using as a walking pole.

A voice nearby said, "Woah there, son."

Paul's throat constricted as he saw the barrel of a rifle pointed at him. Then a figure emerged from the trail. The man holding the gun was tall, rugged-looking with shaggy hair poking out of the edges of his hat. His eyes were dark and curious as they swept over Paul, taking in the tattered gray, too-short pant legs and borrowed too-big coat.

"Where you headed?" the man asked languidly, lowering the gun's barrel.

Paul swallowed. "Up," he said and jerked his head in the direction of the trail.

"Little late in the season to be hiking for pleasure."

"I'm hunting," Paul said.

The man eyed him carefully. "Where's your weapon?"

"I..." Paul stumbled over the next words. "I lost it. Took a tumble and it fell."

"Well now, that's a shame," the man said. He looked up the trail that Paul was headed toward. "Looks like you ain't dressed quite right for the elements." He pointed to the knapsack which, Paul realized, had a large, and very visible white label on the top that said, "Vermont State Hospital for the Insane."

"It's my day off. Thought I'd get out in the woods once more before the weather turns bad."

The man stared for a moment. Was he contemplating taking Paul with him, back down the mountain? Calling the authorities?

Seeming to have decided, the man held out his free hand. "Barker."

"Paul," Paul said and shook the man's calloused hand.

"You planning on staying out here long?"

"No. No, just a day or two."

Barker either laughed or coughed, it was hard to tell which. "There's snow up ahead. Top's already dusted and there's more coming. Looks like the little drought is over, huh?" Barker paused but Paul didn't say anything.

"Mark my words, you won't get in another day before the snow flies thick and heavy. Up here?" He motioned to the woods with the butt end of the rifle. "At this elevation, you'll find that Mother Nature doesn't hold back. I can smell it in the air."

Paul frowned but nodded. Snow? He wasn't prepared for that. He followed Barker's gaze down to his own feet. Clad in the thin boots he'd gotten at the asylum, they were not hiking wear and Barker seemed about to mention it.

Instead, the tall man merely nodded. "Well, good luck to you."

"You too," Paul said. "See any deer?"

Barker shook his head, then spit a long, thin line of tobacco juice into the leaves underfoot. "I ain't hunting deer."

"No? Bear then?"

"Nah. Too late in the season. I'm looking for something else."

Barker looked at Paul, a question in his eyes. *He knew. He'd seen it too.* But Paul, face deadpan said nothing. "Oh. Well, safe travels, Barker."

"Same to you, son. You be careful out there."

Barker turned and was quickly closed up by the undergrowth minutes later.

Paul exhaled and turned back to the trail. His legs ached. Blisters were forming on his feet. And in the short time, he'd stopped to talk to Barker, he'd started to lose body heat. He pulled his coat closed, buttoned it, and started walking again.

IT WAS PAST SUNSET by the time Paul made camp. He'd been lucky to find an area where the ground was somewhat flatter than the rest of the trail he'd come up. Was it the same area where they'd made camp that first night? Paul didn't think so. He'd walked longer.

He pictured for a moment crawling into the canvas tent that he and Jane had put up that night. Feeling her warm, soft body next to his...an ache formed in his throat. He distracted himself by looking for pine boughs which he fashioned a makeshift shelter and started a small fire. It was just enough to warm parts of his body in turn: first his hands, then his feet, his legs, arms, and back. He'd eaten the stolen eggs for breakfast and now broke off a small piece of the cheese and bread. These would spoil before the apples, so he'd save those for Jane, along with the cookies. Jane liked ginger cookies.

He drank sparingly from the canteen and watched the flames hiss and pop. The hissing came from the still-damp wood and leaves he'd found. These made more smoke than he'd like, but he didn't have a lot of other options. He kept other branches near the fire, leaned up in a teepee, and turned them every so often. This way, they'd dry and he'd have a better fire later.

Paul felt his eyes growing heavy. He blinked and yawned. The flames licked at the wood and cast dancing shadows on the trees beyond where Paul sat. His eyes grew heavier and heavier. Finally, he fell asleep with a small bite of bread still in his mouth. He dreamt of Jane and icy branches and white feet running over a dark, cold forest floor. A noise tangled in the dark dreams.

Paul woke with a start. The bread he'd had in his mouth before drifting off clung to the inside of his cheek like a wet slug. He swallowed it down, listened. He'd heard something but was it a cry from someone in his dream or something here in the forest? Had he heard branches breaking? A howl? He sat up, the air was frigid. The fire had burned low and he stoked the coals with a stick, then carefully added the nearly-dry branches from the teepee, blowing on the coals until the flames hungrily licked the wood.

He scrubbed his hands over his arms. His breath came in white puffs as he listened. For several minutes he heard nothing other than the noises of the woods at night. Far away an owl hooted. Branches creaked and groaned overhead. Was that what had woken him? He closed his eyes so that he could hear more deeply.

Then he heard something different. A grunt and then a shuffle. Something large, moving through the undergrowth. Paul found the flashlight—it had slipped beneath his knapsack—and shone it where the sound was coming from. The branches in the undergrowth swayed slightly but he didn't see anything else. No dark fur. No shaggy head or wide, square-yellow teeth. No golden eyes. A shudder ran through his body.

It was quiet in the woods again for several long minutes. The fire popped. A branch overhead creaked once, twice, three times. Then, the grunting sound came again, yards from where it had been. Closer to Paul. He stood up, flicked the light in that direction. The blanket fell away and cold air hit him like a wall. Paul focused on the noise, trying to track it through the darkness.

There it was again.

A rustling. Louder. Closer.

Another grunt, this one louder, deeper. Then a different sound. Something like a stick being rubbed on another stick.

Then the sound of something crashing through the underbrush. The flashlight jerked in Paul's hand. He crouched, grabbed for the poker stick. His heart thundered in his chest, his breath came in jagged puffs.

A small buck leaped into the undergrowth on the other side of the trail. His eyes in the beam of the flashlight were wide with surprise. He gave a final grunt and then leaped into the nearby brush. His white tail bobbed in the light until Paul lowered it to the ground. He sat by the fire and re-wrapped himself in the blanket. His hands were damp with sweat, his limbs shaking slightly.

He laughed a little, weakly, and kept his eyes open. If he closed them he knew what he'd see. The creature. The beast with the golden eyes. Everything he'd felt when he'd first woken from his feverish state at the asylum came rushing back.

The sky was turning the palest shade of pearl gray when he opened his eyes next. His teeth chattered and his hands shook. His fingers were nearly numb and his breath came in great, white clouds as he packed the blanket and flashlight. He longed for coffee or a bowl of hot oatmeal. Hot anything. Instead, he took a swig of water and felt it slide down into his empty stomach.

He'd feel better once he was moving.

IT TOOK SIX MORE HOURS of hiking to get to the cave. More than once along the trail, Paul worried that he'd missed it. That he hadn't seen the cave's entrance through the pine trees that dotted the woods here, or the undergrowth that was tangled with dead leaves. The cave was positioned off the trail after all, easy to overlook. He'd always had a good sense of direction. But this was different. He'd been on Shiny Creek Trail only once before and then, he'd had a map.

Paul stopped to take a swig of water. He remembered that night when they'd first come here. He'd gone into the back of the cave, looking for water. And he'd found it. A large, icy cold brook at the bottom of a sharp ravine. He'd filled the canteens before turning and seeing something that had made his blood turn as cold as the mountain water.

A black fog seemed to roll off the cave wall. A scratching, scrabbling sound like claws over stone. The fog or mist had started to take shape then, forming itself into something that resembled a figure. Paul hadn't waited to see. Instead, he'd run from the ravine, clambering up the stones and bumping and bashing his way back to the entrance of the cave. He'd been frantic to find Jane. To make sure his friends were all right.

Only, once he'd reached the light of the campfire, and had seen Deidre and Allan sleeping peacefully, he'd started to question himself. Had he really seen the mist or just imagined it? He'd been tired—so tired—that it had been easy to talk himself out of what he'd seen. He wished now that he'd said something, that he'd tried to tell Allan and

Deidre. Had warned them. And that he'd been able to find Jane that night in the woods...

Now, Paul stood in front of the cave, sweating and out of breath. His heart pounded hard under his rib cage. It wasn't all from the exertion of the climb.

He was here. Back where he never wanted to be.

He'd returned to the cave where everything had begun.

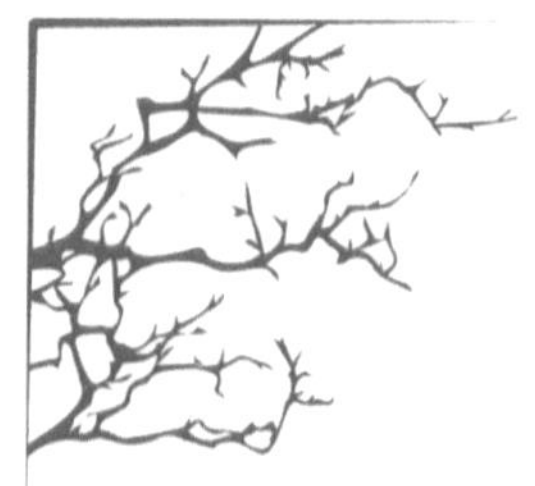

# Chapter Six

"WHERE'S JANE?" PAUL'S voice jerked Allan out of a thick, black sleep. It took Allan a few seconds to remember where he was. The hike. The trail. The cave. He rolled over, opened his eyes, and looked around.

"She uh, she went out to the bathroom."

Paul stood behind the low-burning fire. How long had Allan been asleep? Paul's arms were loaded with four canteens which he lowered to the ground nearby.

"When was this?" Paul's eyes were furtive, looking around the corners of the cave as though Jane might be hiding there in the shadows.

"Just shortly after you left. I got tired and decided to turn in. She said she'd be right back—"

"Right back? That was forty minutes ago, Allan."

"Forty?" Allan scrubbed a hand over the back of his head and felt the hair stand on end. "Are you sure?"

"Yes, I'm sure," Paul said, his voice low and tight with annoyance. "I timed myself to see how far away the water source was." Then, "I'm going out after her."

Thin fingers of dread poked Allan. He struggled to his feet. "I'll go with you."

"No. Stay here with Deidre."

Without another word, Paul exited the cave. If there had been a door on it, Allan thought wryly, Paul would have slammed it behind him.

Well. How was Allan supposed to have known Jane had been gone that long? Maybe she found a berry bush and was gathering some to bring back with her. Maybe she…maybe she what? It was dark out there, and the wind tore around the sides of the cave in big gusts. It wasn't likely Jane was picking berries or frolicking through the daisies. He snorted at the thought but still felt anger twisting at his insides. It was like Paul to blame him. Accuse him of being irresponsible, when it was Paul's own wife who'd gone out alone in the night. What was Allan, her babysitter?

His head was killing him. He put a hand to his forehead and rubbed. The ache between his eyes had formed soon after they'd set up camp in the cave. It had only grown worse in the hours since. He should put more branches on the fire. It had died down a little.

Instead, he fumbled in his backpack, drew out his flask, and took a long pull. Then he leaned back on his bedroll, his eyes going to the cave ceiling. What was left of the firelight flickered over the planes of the ceiling.

It was strange. In the dimness, it almost seemed that the symbols they'd seen earlier were brighter, not harder to see. As though they were glowing. Allan glanced toward the opening of the cave. Was moonlight coming in? But no, the night was dark. The sky—what little he could see of it from here—was smudged with inky black clouds.

Allan's eyes felt heavy and his head throbbed. He should have thought to bring something. Had Deidre packed their little emergency kit? He thought of rummaging through her bag but was too tired. Lethargically, he lay on the thin mat and let his eyes travel around and around the symbols in the center of the star. It was odd. The symbols seemed to move as his eyes traced them. Allan felt his body relax and his mind loosen. Even the knot of tension in his skull eased slightly. He let out a sigh. A sound wafted through the cave, faintly at first. Like nails scratching against a chalkboard or something metal grinding against stone. He tried to open his eyes and see where the noise was coming from but he was too tired.

*That's right, Allan. Just let go.*

What the—Allan tried to roll over and look at Deidre. Had she said that? But it was a man's voice. No, not quite a man's. It sounded, strangely, like Allan's own voice, but different. Hollowed out. Had he said those words out loud?

He listened intently but didn't hear them again. Maybe it had been the wind. His eyes went back to the ceiling, began to trace the symbols again. He followed them like the hands of a clock: one to two, then two to three, then three to four, four to five....as his eyes tracked the symbols his body relaxed. His brain went quiet. All the frustration he felt started to fall away. The impatience, the knowledge that no one on this trip—no one—cared about this story as much as he did, it all faded. He felt like a child again. Peaceful. Unworried about the future. Who cared what the next few hours held even? He could rest here, safe.

*Do you know how long I've waited for you?* The whispered words were like warm honey coating his brain. This time, Allan didn't try to pinpoint their origin. He just listened.

"No," he said. His voice sounded strange in his own ears.

*So long...* the last word was half-sigh. *I know you came here for answers. I can help you find them. The others don't know or care as much as you, Allan. They aren't driven with the same passion you are. They don't care about success the way you do. It's always been like this, hasn't it? No one else really understands what drives you. But I do.*

"Yes," Allan said, the symbols beginning to move in a blurry circle above him. "Yes, that's true. I've always been misunderstood."

*Of course, you have. Poor Allan. As a boy you learned not to trust your parents—they only wanted to take from you, didn't they? And now...well, now you have Deidre and your work. But does she understand you? Does she want the answers like you do?*

Did Deidre really want the answers? Allan had felt them slipping further and further away. He'd first noticed it months ago. The silence between them grew in places where intelligent conversation had flourished before. The glances—pointed and sharp—when Allan chose his work over the social engagement Deidre set up. Without asking him of course. And the almost frantic way that his wife had of trying to get his attention.

Just look at this trip. While he was working hard, putting up the tent—a top-of-the-line one at that—she'd been playing with ferns and trying to get him to snap photos of her. Deidre was selfish. She could be fun and engaging, entertaining, yes. But only if she were the center of attention.

*Like Beatrice, isn't she?* The words—ones he'd avoided maybe since he'd met Deidre—spun through his mind. No. No, she wasn't anything like that his mind halfheartedly offered. But already this new, stronger voice was encouraging him to look deeper. To look closer. Just like Beatrice, Deidre had to be the center of attention. Had to be in the limelight.

Beatrice. His older sister could do no wrong. While Allan brought home good grades, Beatrice brought home perfect grades. While Allan dated nice girls, Bea married the Valedictorian of her high school. She settled into a life of ease where she doted on her doctor husband, while Allan—defiant for the first time in his life—went on to school for photography and journalism. His parents were, "so very disappointed," that he'd decided to "throw his life away," that they'd threatened to cut him out of the will. "No Warning has ever held a job as a...a journalist," his mother had hissed. His father hadn't said anything, just stood, staring out over their estate by the big windows. But his fingertips had been white against the small glass they were wrapped around.

But that was before. Before his older sister died giving birth to her first child, a stillborn. Even in death, she outdid him. Mentioning her name would cause a film of pain to coat his mother's face, and turn his father to stone. They couldn't, wouldn't talk about Beatrice. The sainted daughter who never did wrong. Unlike Allan. The son who never got it right. Her portrait hung, draped in flowers and a rosary in their bedroom. If only...their longing looks said. If only it had been him instead of her.

*That's right, Allan. And is Deidre so different? She always needs to be center stage while you take her photograph and stay in the shadows. She's not even true to you. What about Ralph?*

Allan would have groaned if he could remember how. In this strange, molasses-like state he couldn't make his body respond as he wanted.

Ralph. Ralph Johnson, the youngest editor of the paper. The guy was homely but charismatic. When he'd been promoted to managing editor, the few women in the office had taken notice. Lipstick was more regularly freshened, skirts worn a tad bit shorter, blouses a little lower cut. He'd accused Deidre of doing the same one night after a few too many bourbons.

*And she'd denied it all*, the voice whispered. *But can you really trust her?*

Could he? Allan thought back to the other times: the flirting, the dancing, the gay, happy laughter that spilled from Deidre's mouth only when they were at a dance or when she was chatting with some new "friend" in their circle. Some friend of a friend—always male—made Deidre's eyes a little brighter, her laughter last a little longer.

*You remember what happened at the picnic, don't you, Allan?* Allan wanted to put his hands over his ears, to burn the memory of the picnic from his brain. *Go on,* the voice slithered through his brain cells. *Go on.*

And Allan couldn't stop the images from coming. Like an underground spring hit during a dig, they gushed to the surface. Deidre walking into the woods with Larry Polk, a senior editor at the company picnic. Allan, a bit boozy, had watched with a half-smile, pausing in his own flirty conversation with the new typist whose name he couldn't remember. He'd forgotten about Deidre and Larry for a while, his attention on the typist who was pretty and young with soft-looking blonde curls and wide, blue eyes. She'd said something witty and he'd touched her shoulder. He'd gotten them more drinks.

Then, later they'd danced. A musical trio had come to play ragtime tunes and he'd offered his hand to the typist and they'd swung and shimmied and glided around the grassy dancefloor above the sandy beach. He'd pressed her body—lithe and supple—against his own, smelled the sweet, cloying scent of her hair.

And later, when Deidre had reappeared, alone, from the woods, she'd looked wrong somehow. Askew. Guilty. Allan couldn't pinpoint it at the time but now it was so obvious. She'd been with Larry. She'd gone off into the woods and—

*Yes,* the voice encouraged. *She went off and humiliated you. Made a mockery of your marriage. She doesn't love you, Allan. She never has. You've been little more than a plaything to her. Someone who had money and a new car and a life she wanted.*

Allan felt physical pain in his chest, radiating from his heart across his sternum.

*You mean nothing to Deidre. You're not good enough. She doesn't want you.*

The words, "doesn't want you," echoed around in Allan's head like a gunshot's retort. He crumpled suddenly, drawing his knees to his chest. Humiliated, he felt hot salty rivers of tears tracking down his face. He hadn't cried since he was an eleven-year-old boy and his grandfather had died. He didn't cry when Beatrice died, instead pushing the tears into bitter pieces and shoving them down, far down inside of him.

*You'll never be good enough for Deidre. Just like you were never good enough for your parents. They didn't want you either, Allan. Only Beat-*

*rice.* The voice sighed these words out, as though telling them with great sadness.

The pain in Allan's heart now radiated throughout his entire chest. His whole body began to tingle and ache with it. It felt hot and sour, this anger. No, more than anger. Rage. Fury.

*Of course, you feel that way,* the voice soothed. *Why not make it right?* The voice was silky smooth against the hot, sharp pains in his head. It felt cooling, like silk ribbons over a pebbled driveway.

But how?

*Teach Deidre a lesson.*

Why not? His pride was already shattered. His heart was breaking in two. Why not share some of this pain with his wife? It was her fault, after all. Her lies, her deception, her unfaithfulness. He hadn't broken their marriage vows. Sure there'd been a few dalliances here and there, but he was, after all, a man. Those things were to be expected and none of them had mattered.

But Deidre. Sweet, beautiful Deidre. She was his wife. His. Wife. She was meant for him and him alone. How dare she throw everything he'd ever given her back into his face? How dare she be so ungrateful?

*Yes, how dare she?* the voice whispered.

"But what should I do?" Allan was surprised at the sound of his voice, reedy and thin and not at all like his usual deep tenor. "How should I teach her a lesson?"

*Oh, I have some ideas.*

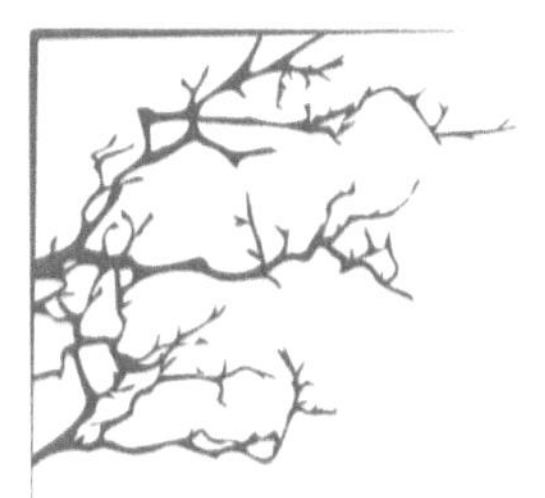

# Chapter Seven

*Paul Rogers*
*Thursday, November 8, 1917*
*Shiny Creek Trail*

"JANE? JANE...ARE YOU here?" *Here, here, here:* the words echoed back from the damp stones. Paul paused, his hand pressed against the stone wall. He was tired. His feet ached from stumbling over the dank, jagged rocks and stones. He'd poked and prodded, investigated, and looked around every boulder, every pile of stones.

Nothing.

No trace of Jane or anything else—human or animal—occupying the space.

Paul pushed himself away from the wall. She could be further back. How far did this cave go? It felt like he'd been walking for hours, but had probably been only one, maybe a little more. His stomach pinched painfully. His throat was dry. The rest of the water had run out. He licked his lips and considered. Maybe exploring the area where the brook ran made more sense. If he was living here, he'd want to be close to the water.

He shivered suddenly. Living here. Could Jane have survived all these weeks here, in this place? Turning, Paul moved to the left, following the sound of rushing water. It was more muted than when he was here last. The past couple of months had been abnormally dry—something that had been the topic of many conversations among the staff at the asylum—and Paul guessed that the brook was experiencing the effect.

He was right. As he made his way carefully down the slope of the ravine with the flashlight between his teeth, he could see the banks of the brook below. He shone the beam to the right and the left. Boulders, rocks, and stones covered nearly every inch. The water had previously lapped the edges of the rocks and in some places spilled over to submerge them. Now, a thick layer of silt lay between the brook and the stones.

His throat was so dry, he didn't even bother fishing his canteen out of the pack, just crouched over the brook, the tips of his boots in the water, and brought water in great handfuls to his face. It was frigid, turning his insides to ice, but he didn't stop until he felt slightly nauseous. He stood, letting the water settle more completely in his empty stomach. He was about to pull his pack from his shoulders when he saw something.

From the corner of his eye, he could see an indentation in the silt. Maybe an animal's tracks? He shone the light over it. His heart stumbled in his chest before rapidly galloping on. It was a footprint. No, it was a line of footprints. The beam of light traced over the indentations. They ran from the water's edge to the rocks and boulders nearby where they disappeared.

But they were very much human. And small enough to be a woman's.

"Jane?" Paul called, his voice bouncing off rocks and stones. He stumbled forward, following the prints until they ran out. "Jane, where are you? Jane?"

*Jane, Jane, Jane,* his voice echoed.

She was here. She had to be here.

Paul fumbled along the stones and rocks along the ravine, not going up but sideways. He moved slowly, excruciatingly slowly, looking for any sign that another human had been here. A single strand of hair, a button, another footprint, a piece of lint. Anything.

But he found nothing.

An hour later, Paul sank onto a rock. The cold crept under his pants but he barely noticed. With his head propped in his hands, elbows resting on his knees, he listened to his jagged breath.

His legs burned and ached and his shoulders were rubbed raw from the straps of the knapsack. He needed a plan. Needed to stop this willy-nilly search he'd been conducting and create a strategy.

What were the options? He could continue this way, looking for more prints. Or go back and make camp for the night near the cave's opening. There it was flat and there was room for a fire. Paul knew he had to get warm. Hypothermia wasn't just possible in a snowstorm, but a risk in damp, cold places, too. He didn't want to go back though. He was so close. Jane might be just around the next corner, or just a bit further back.

But why wasn't she answering him? His throat was raw from yelling her name.

He knew what he needed to do but his heart wrenched in his chest thinking about it. He had to take care of himself. He'd been hiking and stumbling around in this cave for hours. He was exhausted, his body fatigued, his thought processes slowing. Hunger was a constant ache in his belly. What good would he be to Jane if he collapsed somewhere in exhaustion?

Slowly, Paul heaved himself up from the rock and went back the way he'd come. As he passed the footprints in the silt again, he knelt and traced a bootprint with his finger. He had an idea.

Standing, he found a sharp stick and in careful letters, wrote in the thick muck:

"Jane, it's Paul. I'm at cave entrance. I love you."

He stood back to look at his work. If she came back, she'd see the note. Maybe it would be just a few hours. He smiled at the thought and it fueled his long, painful walk back to the cave's entrance.

A TWIG SNAPPED IN THE fire and sent a flurry of sparks upward. Paul leaned back against the rock behind him. He'd eaten—just a little—and had more to drink and now he felt dozy. What he wouldn't do for a bottle of brandy or even a single glass. The thought of the warm liquid flowing down his throat and easing the aches and pains in his body was like a Siren song. He dropped his head to the boulder beneath him, grateful for a pillow even if it was a hard stone one.

He'd avoided looking at the strange symbols above him so far. Even now here in the light and warmth of the fire, he had shivered when he'd glanced at them earlier. There was something about them...something dark. A pressing feeling that was hard to put into words. For a journalist, he should be embarrassed that the words wouldn't come. The closest he could get was ominous.

Pulling the blanket a little tighter, he thought again about the footprints. For the first time in a long time, he felt hope stirring in his heart. He'd wanted to believe she was alive. He'd hoped it and dreamt of it. The chances weren't good though. A single woman, alone in the wilderness without food. How long could she survive? But she had. Somehow she had and he'd seen the proof. Soon, soon she would be—

A loud crack of stone against stone broke his reverie.

Paul jerked upright and swiveled, his hand already searching for the flashlight and the walking stick. He shone the light in the direction from which the noise had come. There was nothing there. He stood, letting the blanket fall. It was déjà vu, the same experience from the night before in the forest when he'd been surprised by the buck in rut. But this was no deer. Deer didn't live in caves.

"Jane?" His voice was a hollow whisper, barely audible above the wind that had picked up outside. It moaned around the cave's entrance like a ghost.

"Jane, is that you?" he called a little louder.

And then a figure stumbled out from the darkness. It moved unevenly and slowly, its steps measured and careful on the stones and rocks underfoot. Paul was so shocked that he looked away toward the cave wall, then back again. He blinked. The figure kept moving toward him, slowly, ever so slowly.

It was a woman. Her head was bent forward, stringy hair hiding her face. Her hands and forearms were covered in scratches and bruises. She was thin—painfully thin—and as Paul moved toward her, a rancid, foul odor filled his nostrils.

He didn't care. He stumbled toward her, tripping over rocks, not looking where he was going. She lifted her face, her eyes like hollow sockets, her cheeks caved in and gaunt. Her skin was covered in dirt and grime. Small twigs and what looked like old leaves were caught in her lank hair.

"Jane?" he moved more slowly now like he was approaching a flighty horse or a skittish dog. "Jane, it's me. It's Paul."

The eyes stared back dully.

Finally, "P-P-Paul?" a voice came from lips that were cracked.

Paul realized at that moment that he'd made a mistake. The voice wasn't that of his wife.

"Deidre," he said quietly.

She raised her hands toward him.

"Paul? Paul?" Then she was crying, great choking sobs that shook her whole frame. "Paul. Paul, you came." The words fell out in halting gasps between breathless sobs.

She clung to him, her hands surprisingly strong, her fingers digging into his flesh painfully. He held her, patted her back as though she was a frightened child. He made shushing noises and held her that way for several long minutes. Finally, she quieted, the sobs coming now in smaller, hitching breaths.

"Deidre. Come sit by the fire. I have food and water. Come with me. You're safe now."

"Safe," she said the word in disbelief.

"Safe," he repeated. He led her to the fire, settled her into his spot, covering her with the scratchy blanket. Then he dug into the pack for some of the bread and cheese. She snatched it from his hands and bit into it. She shoved the food into her mouth so quickly that she drew blood from her fingers.

"Slowly, Deidre. You don't want to get sick."

She ignored him, stuffing the rest of the cheese into already full cheeks. She made little huffing noises and grunted as she ate. He looked away, embarrassed. The Deidre he knew would have died of humiliation to be seen this way.

When she'd finished, he offered her the canteen. She sipped a little slowly, clutching it with trembling hands. Her nails were broken and jagged, the varnish long since worn away.

"Why are you...here?" she asked. Her voice was rusty with disuse. She stared at him, the flames casting deeper shadows on the emaciated planes of her face. It looked like a skeleton with skin wrapped over it. He glanced away, into the fire which he poked at needlessly.

"I was looking for you. And Jane."

"Jane," she said, the name a sigh on her lips. She stared into the fire. Her hair hung in limp clumps that she didn't bother to push away. "Jane's gone."

Paul's head snapped up. He looked at Deidre. "Where?"

She ignored him, took another sip of water. Her fingers on the canteen were white-tipped as though she was using a lot of strength to hold onto it.

"Where did Jane go, Deidre?"

She didn't say anything for a moment, just stared into the flames.

"Deidre? Where is she? Please, please tell me."

She sat silently another moment, then raised her eyes to his. The dancing flames made her eyes dark black holes in her face. He could see her eyes glittering out from beneath her browbones.

"She's dead."

When Paul was five, he'd been ice skating with his brother. Paul had tripped over a root on the pond and landed flat on his back. He remembered it clearly still, after all these years. Everything had come into stark relief: the tree branches above him swaying in the breeze; a Blue Jay screeching; then the sound of his brother's voice as he'd skated back toward Paul, very fast. It had been as though not having his breath had accentuated his vision and hearing, making them more powerful. But with it had come the painful, frightening feeling of breathlessness. As though a huge rock had toppled onto his chest and pinned him to the ice.

He felt that now.

A crushing, pressing weight in his chest. His breath was gone.

They sat without speaking for several minutes, both staring unseeingly into the flames. Then a branch popped in the fire and a shower of sparks flew up.

Paul found his voice which sounded flat and dead in his ears. "How?"

Deidre shook her head slowly from one side to the other. "I don't know. I think that thing got her."

"What thing?" Paul asked, turning his head to look once again at Deidre.

She looked back at him, a twisted half-smile on her face. "You know what I mean, Paul. The thing we saw that day. It killed Allan. And it's been chasing me, hunting me. The creature." Her voice faded away. When she spoke again though, it was hard. "The monster in the woods."

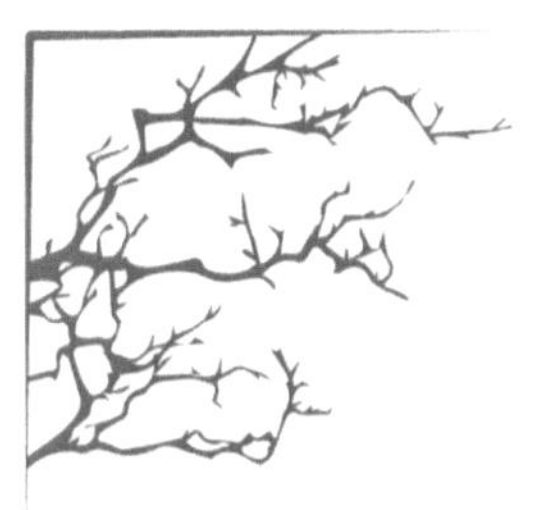

# Chapter Eight

ALLAN CROUCHED BESIDE a large pile of stones, hidden from view. He was far enough from the cave's entrance that what he was about to do wouldn't be heard. Besides, Paul was still out in the windy forest, searching for Jane. The area was dimly lit. Allan glanced over to the cave wall closest to him and noticed dark tendrils of what looked like smoke or fog gathering. They pulled from the wall and drifted toward him.

He fingered the blade of the knife in his hand. Rather than feeling nervous or scared, he felt a cool rush of peace overtake him.

*That's right, Allan. It's because this was meant to be.* The voice said in a silky whisper.

It wasn't a peace like Allan had ever experienced before though. This was laced with excitement. Anticipation. He shut his eyes momentarily and saw again the strange symbols from the ceiling swirling behind his eyelids. Like they'd been implanted there. Like they were part of him now.

He almost laughed in relief. It was as though for the first time in his life, he was free. He knew precisely what needed to be done and was the only one who could do it. And he was prepared. His finger moved over the sharp blade again. He pressed his index finger into it, just a little to test its sharpness. A line of red formed and he felt a small, quick burn of pain. He smiled and moved his finger away.

It was ready.

He was ready.

He'd told Deidre to meet him here. Kissed her awake. Told her that there was something beautiful he'd wanted to show her. She'd roused, her auburn hair tousled around her face, her cheeks pink with sleep. He'd felt a pang then, not of guilt over what he was about to do, but anger over the way he'd loved her. The way he'd given himself to her—all of him—and she had thrown his love and affection aside like refuse.

"Come with me," he'd whispered in her ear, smelling the fragrance she always wore, an expensive perfume that she got each year for Christmas from her parents. "Come and see this. You're not going to believe it, Dee. It's beautiful."

Then, he'd hurried ahead. He'd heard her voice, sleepily calling after him, "Can't it wait till morning, cookie?" but he'd ignored it, pressing on into the darker part of the cave. Hiding behind the boulder. Lying in wait for her.

What was that? A strange scuttling sound filled the air in the dark recesses of the cave beyond where Allan crouched. He looked around but couldn't see anything. He should have brought a flashlight. But then, that would give him away. The scuttling sound got louder, a strange sort of grating noise that he could hear clearly even over the distant roar of the water in the ravine.

Allan shifted his weight, leaned slightly more forward, and closed his eyes. He listened harder. Behind his eyelids flickered the strange symbols. The peace he had felt earlier—the excited whisperings over what he was going to do—had faded slightly. In his chest was a dull ache. Like strong hands were inside him, squeezing his lungs. He frowned, adjusted the knife in his hands.

Then, like a dreamer waking, he saw himself crouching, hiding, preparing to ambush his wife.

His own wife.

*Wait,* he wanted to yell, *what is happening to me?*

What was happening? Allan opened his eyes. The black fog rolled in from the edges of the cave toward him. Thicker now. Waves of it. It started to form into a shape, like the figure of a man, only tall, so tall it nearly touched the roof of the cave far above. Allan blinked, looked again.

The grating sound grew closer. A wash of terror poured over him.

*What was happening? What was happening? What was happening?*

He tried to stand, but his legs were like taffy. He tried to throw the knife to the side but his hand, shaking, was immobilized.

Allan felt the darkness pressing closer before he saw the fog swirl around his legs, then his torso, then his mind. It felt cold—icy—and heavy. At first, he felt afraid. But then, once it had covered him and coated him completely, he felt the same strange peace that he'd felt earlier. This time though, it was mixed with a sense of resignation.

He had to do this.

It was the only way.

She deserved it.

*That's right, she does,* the voice whispered in Allan's ear—no, into his mind—where it slithered like a snake, winding itself around and around in his brain until Allan couldn't think or feel or hear anything else at all.

Just the voice. The honeyed, tangling whispers.

And his own heart, beating out a single word: revenge.

DEIDRE SAT UP, SLEEPILY. Her head felt thick and full like it was filled with pillow stuffing. What time was it? She groaned and stretched her arms over her head. It was chilly in the cave and she shivered as she pulled her sweater closer.

Where was everyone?

She glanced around. The fire was still glowing, casting the same strange shadows on the walls. She avoided looking up. The symbols they'd seen earlier had made a hollow feeling in her stomach.

"Allan?" she called. But there was no answer. The wind was loud outside the cave. She could see tree branches bending and twisting in the dingy light. Where was everybody?

She stood slowly. Her legs ached, her shoulders were sore and her feet felt swollen as she pulled her boots back on. For the first time since they'd started this trip, she wished she hadn't come.

It was supposed to have been a great adventure, something to tell stories about when they got back to the office. Something to impress their colleagues with. Not to mention she and Allan sharing a byline in a national magazine.

"They'll be lining up for us to write for them, pet," Allan had said more than once, a crooked grin on his handsome face. And she'd known it would happen. Allan made things happen. He was a go-getter, her mother always said with admiration in her voice. And didn't he always, always get what he wanted?

But now it all felt too real. The stories they'd researched—about the people who had gone missing here—they'd been distant and far away. Like folk tales or ghost stories, one told around a campfire, they hadn't existed. But now, in this oppressive cave in the middle of nowhere, her body bruised and her head thick, it struck her that those stories were true. The accounts of ordinary people—people just like her and Allan and Jane and Paul.

What if they ended up in a newspaper?

Deidre shivered again and called out, "Allan?"

"Here," his voice sounded far away, tinny in the dank cave. "Come see."

Brandishing a flashlight, Deidre stumbled over rocks and stones toward the interior of the cave. She hadn't been back here, preferring the light and warmth of the fire and the proximity to the outside world. She hummed as she walked, trying to lighten the closeness she felt. It was strange, this cave. The air itself felt weighted, thick. She shivered again.

Where was Allan?

She scanned the cave walls around her with the flashlight but there were only more rocks and boulders and stones of all sizes. They made it hard to balance and so she moved slowly. Then she heard something.

A strange, grating sound filled the air. It sounded like someone running their fingernails over a chalkboard, or like claws scrabbling over rocks. Deidre shone her light around wildly, took a misstep, and nearly fell. She caught herself on a boulder. It felt damp and slimy under her hand. She was about to pull it back when something shot out of the darkness and grabbed it. It gripped her hand tightly.

Deidre screamed and dropped her flashlight. The sound grew louder. It pressed around the edges of the cave, drawing closer to her. The air had turned freezing, as though she'd walked into an old-fashioned ice house. Strange whimpering sounds came from her mouth.

The thing holding her hand squeezed it harder, then jerked her forward. She collided with something taut but fleshy in the dark. She tried to scream again, but no sound came out.

"Where's your playful laughter now, Deidre?" the voice said. It sounded like Allan but not. This voice was strange, guttural. "Isn't this a great adventure?"

The grating grew louder. Then Deidre felt something over her skin. Cold and damp, like a mildewing sheet wrapped itself around her. In the gray dark, she could see something even darker pressing against her, over her. It wound itself around her like a shroud. She gasped and tried to pull her head back. She couldn't. Allan's other hand gripped her hair in a fist cementing her in place.

Allan. But different, his features twisted in hate. Revulsion.

"Allan," she managed to get his name out but rather than a shout, it was a strangled whisper. "Allan, what are you doing?"

He threw his head back, a high-pitched, horrible laugh bouncing around the cave's walls, off stone and dirt and dampness.

"What am I doing? I'm settling the score."

"What...what are you talking about?" Deidre's voice was a little louder now. She felt the floor with one foot, edging her toe around rocks and debris. If she could lift a stone...If she could—but then Allan jerked her head backward. Pain screeched through her scalp and tears rushed to her eyes. She cried out and she felt him relax slightly as he pulled her closer to his chest.

"Remember Larry, Deidre?"

She closed her eyes. Pain radiated from her center outward. She didn't want to remember. Had tried her best not to all these months. She'd gone with him into the woods. The summer work picnic and the evening had been delicious in every way. The air had been soft and scented with flowers. The sky was a perfect teal when Larry had grabbed her hand and inclined his head toward the woods.

"Come here, beautiful," he'd said.

And she'd followed, like stupid sheep or a dumb puppy. Her head had been spinning—too many of the fizzy pink drinks—and she'd giggled when she stumbled over a root.

"Woah. Careful there." Larry's voice had been hushed when they entered the woods. There were paths carved in the brush, meandering and still in the quiet air. A cricket chirped and a single songbird sang intermittently. Then Larry pushed her against a tree. Deidre could still feel the sharp bark pressing into the thin skin covering her backbone. She'd felt dizzy, his lip on hers. It had felt so good.

It was forbidden.

Secret.

Delicious.

Her breath had tangled in her throat, her limbs had grown looser. He smelled of whiskey and cigarettes and his mouth was hard and soft and hot and hungry all at the same time. They'd both laughed breathlessly as his hands had jerked at her clothes. Buttons came loose, one flew off and landed with a soft plop in the leaves nearby. She'd giggled while loosening his belt.

"I've wanted you for so long," he panted against her cheek. She could feel the moist heat of his breath and she'd leaned her head back and looked up. The leaves above danced and swirled until she had to close her eyes. Their time together was wonderful and horrible all in one. It wasn't that she'd meant for it to happen. Hadn't planned on it when she'd carefully applied her cherry-red lipstick that afternoon or shimmied into her favorite pink slip.

And yet, she couldn't deny that she'd found Larry attractive. All the times at work that he'd complimented her on a new dress or the way she'd fixed her hair. The meaningful glances across the smoke-filled room when they had their weekly staff meeting. His pauses by her desk, his eyes tracing her like an artist studying his model.

Larry was everything Allan wasn't. He was older, more mature. He was quiet and thoughtful, studious with a dry sense of humor. His eyes—dark eyes—were penetrating. Like he could see into her mind, read her thoughts. And rather than finding them banal as Allan so often did, revere them. And admire Deidre herself. Just as she was, not as a project to work on or a challenge to conquer.

Later, when it was over, she'd collapsed onto the soft moss under the tree. Larry hadn't sat beside her and held her like she thought he might. He hadn't pressed his lips against her forehead and called her beautiful again. Instead, he'd cleared his throat, fumbled to put his pants back together, and walked off, mumbling about the need to stretch his legs, a cigarette already dangling from his lips. He'd left her there like a crumpled wad of paper he'd finished with.

It was then that the sick feeling in her stomach started. What had she done? Hot and acidic, the guilt pressed against her insides until she wanted to scream or cry. She did neither. What had it been after all but a little foray? It wasn't as though Allan hadn't had his fair share before they were married. Maybe even since.

So, Deidre had gathered herself. Put her buttons back together. Straightened her skirt. Pulled off the ruined stockings and hid them behind a bush. Smoothed her hair. Then stumbled dizzily back toward the sound of the music, the party that was still going on without her.

"I saw you that night. You little slut." Allan's voice was even stranger now. The "s" sounds had a hiss. He pulled her hand up over her head, pinning it to her back. Then Deidre felt something sharp and pointed against her arm. Slowly, Allan traced it down, down from the soft flesh under her forearm to her wrist. She gasped. The sweater she wore and the shirt beneath it ballooned open. Underneath, her bare skin was exposed to the air and cold.

And the knife that Allan held in his hand.

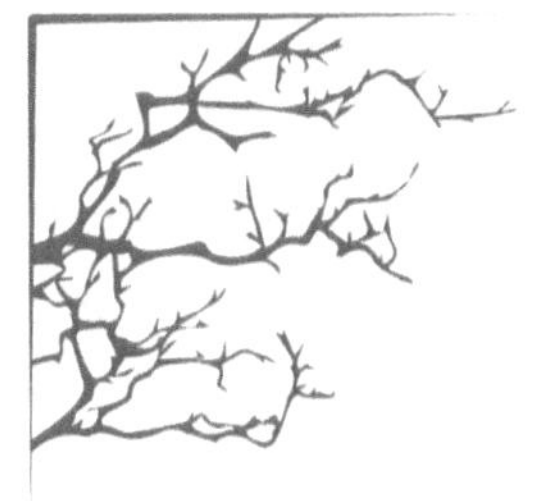

# Chapter Nine

*Paul Rogers*
*Thursday, November 8, 1917*
*Shiny Creek Trail*

PAUL STARED AT DEIDRE. Her words hung over the fire between them. "Monster in the woods." He wanted to tell her to shut up. Wanted to pound his fists into the rock wall. Wanted to run from the cave and never, ever look back.

Had it taken Jane? Was Deidre right and his wife was dead? He felt a hole opening up inside of him, a gaping crevice where his heart used to be.

Jane. Jane. Jane.

He found it hard to breathe. Jane, laughing as he bent his head to whisper something in her ear at the theater. Jane, standing with her dress sleeves rolled up in their kitchen on Christmas morning with flour covering her hands and smudging her cheeks. Jane, lying next to him in their bed, the sun filtering through the wrought iron bars and making a pattern on her smooth white skin. Jane, arriving home from work, tired but asking about his day, offering to mix them drinks.

Jane.

Jane.

Jane.

"No." Paul didn't recognize his voice when he opened his eyes. "No, Deidre, that can't be right."

She was quiet a moment, studying him as though he were the wild one, uncertain of what his next movements might be. Then, "I'm...I'm sorry, Paul."

"But how? You disappeared. They sent a search team, you know, for you and Jane. I read about it in the papers. But they never found anything. How could that be?"

Deidre shook her head slowly. "I don't know." She said the words so softly he barely made them out. "I was here. The whole time. I was too scared to leave. I kept thinking that someone would come. That someone would find me..." Her voice broke then and tears started to run down her cheeks.

She didn't seem to notice. Just stared at the cave's entrance and kept talking. "I should have gone. Should have tried to find the trail again. I could have made it. Might have anyway. I thought maybe Jane was still here. When I came back though, you were both gone. I thought you'd left without me. It was just me. Me and Allan." Her voice stopped with a hitch and a shiver ran through her slight frame. She turned, looked toward Paul again.

"Animals got him you know. He—his body fell after a few days. I brought it outside. It took forever. I put rocks all around it, over it. I tried to bury him, but—"

"Oh God, Deidre, I'm so sorry." Paul moved closer and put a hand out toward her shoulder. She flinched and nearly fell backward off the stone she was using as a chair.

"Sorry," he murmured. He stared into the fire too. He could see her—see Deidre, small and fragile—grasping Allan's arms and pulling him out into the woods. Pictured her sobbing as she built up a makeshift grave for him. Then the animals—wolves? coyotes—coming in the night, howling as they unearthed her husband's body...

He shook his head. "When did you see her last?"

Deidre took another sip from the canteen and flexed her fingers. They were nothing more than bones, her rings jiggling with every motion. The diamond Allan had given her winked in the firelight.

"I don't remember. Every day has blurred into the next one."

"How have you survived, Deidre?" Paul asked, his voice gentler. "How have you managed all this time?"

She shrugged slowly, as though doing so took a lot of effort. "I found some berries and mushrooms. After I finished what was in our packs, I tried to trap an animal, but it didn't work. I don't know if I could have killed it anyway, or with what. I never found Allan's knife. Isn't that strange? I know he had it with him..."

Again her voice drifted away.

Then, "I'm so tired," she said. "Can I sleep here, with you?"

"Of course. Of course, you can. I'm sorry I don't have more to offer than that blanket."

"...salright," her voice was slightly slurred, her head already bending forward on her bony chest. Paul waited until her breath was deeper, evener. Then he positioned her carefully, wrapping the blanket more tightly around her and wedging the pack between her head and the stone she'd rested it on.

He sat and stared into the flames. To survive all those weeks with nothing more than the clothes on your back. And Deidre. Of the four of them, Paul would have guessed her the person least likely to survive such an ordeal. And yet she had.

And Jane hadn't.

She was gone.

Jane was gone.

His beautiful, funny, sweet lovely Jane. The bright light in his life. He put a hand to his mouth to physically push back the sob that was lodged behind his teeth, begging to be released. He wouldn't cry. That was a luxury he couldn't be allowed. Regret boiled inside of him until he thought he'd burst. If only he'd made it back sooner. If only he'd been more lucid when they'd found him, brought him to the hospital. He could have given clearer information, more helpful directions. Paul swore and thumped his fist down on the cave floor. It should have been him! Why had she died and he'd live?

He pushed himself up, strode out of the cave. The walls felt suddenly like a crypt, smothering him, closing in. The air outside was cold but it only made the hot grief in his chest burn brighter. His eyes narrowed and his breath came in slower longer deeper breaths. He had to remain focused. He took all the pain, all the grief inside, and funneled it into one emotion: anger. He had one desire and one only.

To kill the creature that had killed his wife.

PAUL HADN'T EXPECTED to sleep. But when he next opened his eyes, he was perplexed to find himself in the woods. A pair of squirrels argued in the trees above, chattering and hissing at each other. Gray, dull light filled the forest making the bare branches overhead stand out starkly like blackened shards. He sniffed and smelled woodsmoke.

He sat up. His bones ached and his fingers and toes were numb from the cold. He stood. *Deidre.* She must be worried about him, wondering where he'd gone. She might think he'd left her, abandoned her once again. Paul moved as quickly as he could to the fire where she'd been sleeping last night.

She was gone.

The blanket was gone.

So was his knapsack.

The fire had burned down, coals barely winking red.

"Deidre?" he called, his voice pinched and anxious sounding. He coughed, tried again. "Deidre?"

The only sound was the rushing of the water far away and the wind clicking branches together outside. Paul shivered.

Where had she gone?

And—the next thought hit him hard—what was he going to do without any provisions?

He stood at the entrance of the cave for several long minutes, thinking. Two warring voices in his mind.

*You have to get out of the mountains. You have nothing left—no food, no way to make fire—you'll die out here.*

*No, you need to find Deidre. She's all alone.*

*Exposure and hypothermia*, the first voice said.

*Maybe the Bigfoot took her.*

The second voice won. Paul built up the fire, stoking it with more branches until it blazed hot and orange. He stood by it for several long minutes, taking care to warm every part of himself, especially his feet. Frostbite was most likely to happen there or on his fingers. He looked around the campfire for something, anything that would be useful to him. The walking stick he'd been using lay near a boulder. Near it was another branch, shorter and thicker. Paul picked it up and sniffed it. It was pine and—he was in luck—the end that had broken free from the tree was covered in hardened pine pitch. This sap was flammable. Not enough to make a blazing torch, but it would help him see a little better.

The rear of the cave looked as it had the day before. Rocks filled most of the cavern along with dampness and a dank, earthy smell. Paul avoided looking at the spot where Allan's body had swung that day. Instead, he kept his gaze forward. Periodically, he would call out, "Deidre?" but as he moved further into the cave stopped. If that thing had her, he didn't want to bring attention to himself. Surprise might be his best—his only—weapon.

He listened carefully, feeling like he'd morphed into a mole. The cave had a surprising number of noises, all deadened and hollow sounding. There was the muted thrum of the water in the ravine and periodically, the scrabbling of little feet over rocks and leaves. Paul tried to get a better view of whatever was causing the noise but his weak torch didn't throw enough light. It wasn't so much curiosity as hunger that drove his interest. If he were able to snare an animal, he could use the fat for another torch, a better one. His mouth watered at the thought of golden meat roasting over a fire.

He walked. And walked. It felt as though he'd been going for hours, but when he glanced at his wrist the watch face told him it had been closer to fifty minutes. Paul paused, resting on a large, flat stone, his head in his hands. He'd propped the makeshift torch in a crevice between two rocks.

What was he doing? This tunnel could go back for miles. Maybe this cave was part of a mine at some point. Most of it went deep underground, not like the shallow caves on his family's farm. Even if he could find Deidre—and that was a big if—how could he fight off that huge monster with a torch and walking stick? The idea was laughable.

Paul felt a deep sense of despair wash over him.

*That's right, Paul. You've done all you can.*

He righted himself.

Who had said that?

He glanced around, looking for movement, for another human standing nearby. The voice had been slippery smooth, human but not quite. He jabbed the torch around into the darkness. Here, he noticed, the air seemed inkier, more oppressive. Around the edges of the cave, blackness seemed to roll off the walls in little waves, like fog. Paul remembered suddenly the feeling, the presence down by the water when he'd been filling the canteens. He had seen this same strange fog then.

Paul shivered. When had it gotten so cold? Was the exposure to the campfire just now starting to leak out of his system, or had the cave itself dropped in temperature? Goosebumps broke out on his arms and legs.

*You must think of yourself, Paul. There is nothing left here for you. Go home.*

The word "home" shimmied off rocks and stones. Now, the iciness of the air made it hard to breathe. Paul felt his shoulders instinctively hunching as he tried to keep warmth in. He shook his head.

"No." He spoke the word aloud and it was louder than he'd expected. "No, I'm not going home. I'm going to find my friend and help her."

He didn't know what he expected the thing to answer but there was only a long, heavy silence.

Then it spoke again. *Pity.*

Paul shook his head, the frustration he'd been feeling building in his chest until he felt he'd explode from the pressure. He yelled, brandished the torch, and ran wildly to the nearest side of the cave. He shoved the light toward the darkness. It seemed to shrink away, pull back against itself, the fog re-attaching itself to the cave wall. He ran to the other side, skirting larger boulders and bounding off of smaller ones, and did the same thing. Again, when the light got close the dark shrank back.

"I'm not afraid of you," he said, his voice booming in the low tunnel. "Do you hear me? Everything I love is gone. I'm not afraid of what you can do to me."

*Me, me, me* echoed against the stones and bounced over rocks away from him and then back. He pulled out the silver cross that lay against his chest, brandished it along with the torch. Then he turned in a long, slow circle, his thumb rubbing against the phrase there. "The light shines in the darkness, and the darkness did not comprehend it." He spoke the words aloud, first in a regular voice, then louder, and louder and louder still until he was shaking with exertion as he shouted the words into the blackness around him.

Jane had given him the necklace on their first wedding anniversary. Paul wasn't sure what to think about it then and had even felt a little embarrassed by the gift. He wasn't a religious man and Jane knew it.

"It's from the Bible," she'd said, slipping the necklace over his head. The cross lay on a sturdy leather string. "They're good words, Paul," she'd kissed his cheek that morning. "Whether you believe in them or not."

He'd mumbled a thanks into her hair, nuzzled his face into her neck which was sweet and soft.

He stopped yelling now, his voice hoarse. His breath came in great, gulps—half from exertion and half from fear.

He paused.

Listened.

But the voice didn't speak again.

All Paul could hear as he picked up his stick and started forward again was the distant drum of the water far below and the *drip, drip, drip* of water on stone somewhere ahead of him.

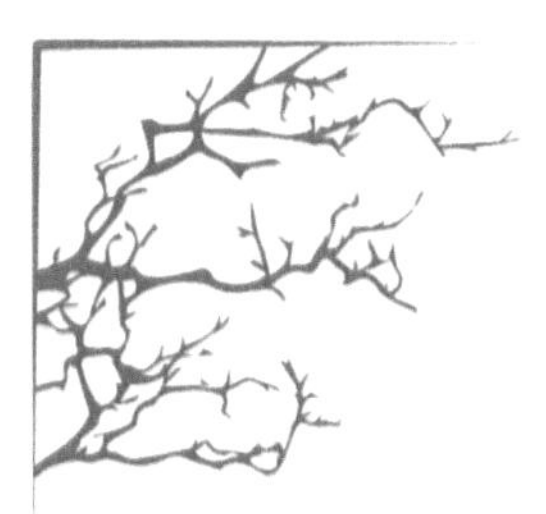

# Chapter Ten



*Deidre Warning*
*Saturday, September 8, 1917*
*Shiny Creek Trail*

DEIDRE TRIED TO SCREAM but only a kitten-like mewling came from her mouth. Allan pressed the flat blade of the knife against the vulnerable flesh of her underarm.

"Allan, why are you doing this?" Deidre's voice was barely more than an agonized whisper. "I'm—" her voice cracked. Allan's hand stopped moving. "I'm your wife."

"You went with him," he said after a moment's hesitation. "I saw you following him into the woods. I should have gone after you. Should have caught you in the act, humiliated you the way you did me."

"I didn't," Deidre said and began to cry. Hot, salty wetness coated her cheeks. Allan's breath was sour and stale. The hand holding the knife trembled slightly. "I didn't mean to."

She heard something then. The same, strange sort of scratching she'd heard earlier. Only, before it had been quiet, more of an annoyance. Now it was loud in her ears. She wanted desperately to cover them, block out the sound. But Allan tightened his grip. Her scalp was on fire, her lips pulled back in a grimace.

"You'll have to pay for what you've done, now." Allan pushed the blade into the soft flesh of her underarm and Deidre cried out in pain.

White-blue explosions formed in front of her eyes as the searing burn extended toward her elbow. She tried to scream, tried to jerk her arm away, but couldn't.

He was going to kill her. Carve her like a chicken, she thought. "Help. Please, someone, help me!"

Allan whispered something unintelligible and withdrew the blade from her arm. A black mist swirled around his hand as he danced the knife in front of her face. Her eyes widened in terror.

She tried to scream. Instead, a moan of hysteria came from her throat.

And then Deidre heard another sound. It was quiet at first but grew louder within seconds. A heavy *huh-huh-huh*, like an animal: big and warm and panting. Deidre glanced wildly in the direction of the sound. A bear? A mountain lion? There was something—a shape, large and looming—over Allan's shoulder. She could barely make it out. Allan's hand still gripped her hair so hard she felt cross-eyed as she struggled to catch a glimpse of whatever was making the noise.

Allan must have heard it too. Recognizing that something wasn't right, he loosened his grip on her and turned to look in the same direction she was. For a moment there was silence. And then, suddenly, Allan let go of her. He'd had a change of heart, she thought at first, nearly collapsing onto the big boulder nearby. But then Allan gave a terrific yell and fell away from her. No, not fell. Was flung. The thing—the Bigfoot that she'd seen in the forest—stood over Allan's crumpled body. She stared at it. Her mind tried and failed to put together things that didn't work. A beast, seven-feet tall—eight?—shaggy and lank-armed, stood over the body of her prone husband. The *huh-huh-huh* was louder now, and a strange, wild smell filled the air. The beast stood looking down at Allan.

It was the blood dribbling and dripping down her arm that finally brought Deidre to her senses.

The monster had killed Allan.

It would kill her, too.

She turned, clutched her arm.

And ran.

DEIDRE WASN'T SURE how long she ran, but when she stopped she was in a thick grove of pine trees. She'd found light in the dark tunnel, followed it to the side of the cave where it had spit her out into the woods.

She bent over, hands on knees, gasping for air. Tears ran down her face and mixed with sweat and mud. Scratches covered her arms and probably her face too, from the sharp branches whipping back as she'd plunged through the woods. Her arm ached where it was sliced. She forced herself to inspect it, moaning as she saw the blood and the separated skin. Nausea swept over her. Deidre took several deep breaths. She could not faint. She could not faint here.

"It's not so bad," she whispered out loud, leaning against a tree. Her stomach roiled. "It will be all right. It's not so bad." She repeated it over and over, like a mantra—*not so bad*—as she sank to the ground, her back against the tree she'd been leaning on.

The air was surprisingly warm, sunlight dappled leaves overhead made a canopy like yellow stained glass. Deidre sat, watching the leaves, her mind working through what had just happened.

Allan...was he dead? A sob rose in her throat and escaped. She put a hand over her mouth, as though physically trying to hold more in. Why had he done that to her? They'd both had their interests in the opposite sex over the years. They were both flirts and yes, sometimes it went beyond just words.

Deidre had never actually slept with anyone else since their marriage. Not until Larry. But even so, Allan had never reacted like this.

She'd never felt afraid of him, afraid he'd hurt her. Mostly, he just shrugged off her flirtations, told her she'd be sorry when he—not she—was named the Pulitzer Prize-winning journalist. "You gotta keep your focus, pet," he'd tell her, snapping his fingers. "You've gotta keep your eyes on the prize, see?"

A branch creaked overhead and Deidre looked around her suddenly. Was it here? That thing from the cave...had it followed her? A cold feeling of dread washed over her. She looked around, expecting to see its massive head, to see its strange, too-long arms and hunched posture between the branches of the copse of trees nearby.

But nothing was there.

Deidre wiped her face and blew her nose on a damp handkerchief from her pocket. She pulled up the legs of her bloomers. Her stockings were torn underneath. She yanked at them, ripping them off at the knees. Then she carefully wound them around her upper arm, making a delicate bandage. Hopefully, it would be enough to staunch the blood.

What now? Return to the cave? She should warn Jane and Paul about Bigfoot, the creature. And what about Allan? What if he was still alive? What if he *was* still alive? Would he turn on their friends the way he had her? There had been something otherworldly about him. His voice...it was like it wasn't him speaking at all but someone—or something—else. And the black mist that had covered him, had seemed to come from him.

She started to shiver, partly from the leftover fear and adrenaline, partly from the new revelation. Something was here with them in the woods. And it was hunting them.

JANE HAD CIRCLED BACK to the cave. At least, she thought she had. But when she entered it was all wrong. The fire that had been glowing hot was gone. No packs littered the floor, bedrolls, or anything else she recognized. Instead, there was only silence and the smell of thick, dark earth in the air.

She sank onto a stone, tried to clear her head. Had she gotten turned around?

Thinking of it—the thing she'd heard behind her in the forest made fingers of fear dance up her spine. She should have...

What?

Should have stayed? Been killed by the Bigfoot?

If it had even been that. She'd never know now because she'd turned tail and run, like a scared rabbit. It had sounded the same though, hadn't it? She closed her eyes, tried to picture the moment in the forest with Deidre. She'd been so frightened that everything had seemed as though it was happening a long way off. Like she had been watching it through a tunnel or peering at the situation through a tele-scope. Around the edges of her memory was a pulsing fear—terror—at what they'd seen.

It couldn't be. It just couldn't be true.

Jane thought then about the newspaper clippings. The ones about the hunters who'd spotted something, some creature right here in these woods. No one had believed them. But what if there was something here in the forest? What if the Bigfoot or monster or whatever it was, had taken James Smithfield all those years ago? Was it responsible for the other disappearances? Did it feed on humans?

Jane straightened on the rock, her head raising an inch, her shoul-ders lifting. One thing was certain. Running panicked through the for-est wasn't going to help. If there was a creature—and yes, despite not wanting to believe it she'd seen it with her own eyes—then her friends could be in danger. Paul could be in danger.

A cold fist of fear knocked into her ribs.

Paul.

Where was he?

She had to get back to the cave—the right cave—and find him.

*Please God, let him be safe.*

Jane got up and smoothed a hand over her clothes. Then she found a thick, sturdy branch with a pointed end. It would work as a weapon in a pinch.

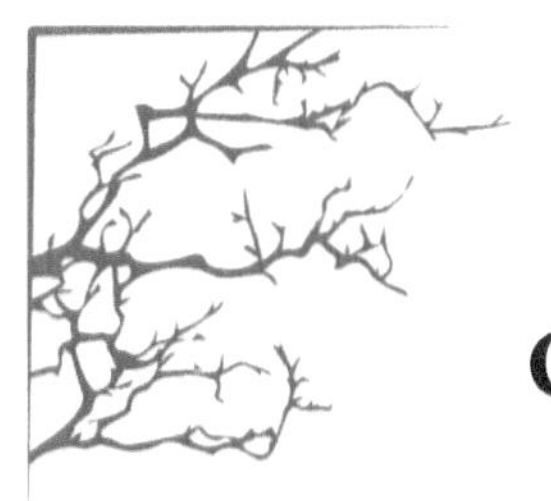

# Chapter Eleven

*Paul Rogers*
*Friday, November 9, 1917*
*Shiny Creek Trail*

PAUL HAD COME TO A "v" deep in the cave. If he turned left, he'd continue down another tunnel. Right—he strained his eyes and head—right might empty into the forest. Light spilled from that direction and everything in him yelled at him to go that way. But he hesitated.

Just a little further. He'd go just a little further and then he'd come back. Take the right-hand turn and leave the cave.

For good.

He stopped for a minute, rested on a big boulder. Unlacing his boots, Paul pulled his damp socks free to survey the damage. His feet had been hurting for hours and now he could see why. Blisters had formed and popped, leaving his skin raw and red in several places. He shook his head, replaced his socks and boots. There wasn't anything he could do for them right now. His feet and legs protested as he restarted walking.

Just a little further. Every hundred feet or so he stopped and listened: for sounds of Deidre or that creature moving about. But there had been nothing so far. Nothing other than the voice in the inky darkness earlier. His mind drifted as he maneuvered around stones and across boulders. His thoughts returned to Jane. Always Jane.

He continued on.

Then, suddenly, he saw something. A strange yellowish light appeared faintly to his right. He blinked slowly. Was he seeing things? He closed his eyes for several long seconds but when he reopened them he still saw the light. What was it? A hole in the cave's ceiling? The ground was higher here and the tunnel he'd walked through emptied into a cavern. The light though was coming from a higher spot. He squinted slightly. It wasn't quite at ceiling height, but close to it, maybe three-quarters of the way up the cave wall.

He moved toward it instinctively. In the dimness of the cave, it likely looked brighter than it was. Then he heard something. It sounded like...no, that wasn't possible. He listened, holding his breath so that he could hear better. It sounded like a woman's voice. Humming.

Paul crept slowly toward the light, sticking to the edge of the cave. The damp coldness rolled off of the wall, coating him. He was getting close now. Thirty feet maybe? In the light, he could see shadows moving. As though someone was in front of it, their motions causing shifts in the beam.

Twenty feet.

The humming was getting louder. It was a tune he recognized but couldn't place. It sounded almost like—no, it couldn't be—but it sounded almost like Jane's voice.

Fifteen feet.

Paul swallowed, took a deep breath, and brandished the walking stick in front of him. Could that thing be making such a human noise? Or was it Deidre? Had she gotten this far away?

He sagged suddenly against the cave wall. That had to be it. Deidre, shining the flashlight, perhaps unpacking the last of the food rations or sipping from the canteen and casting shadows out from the ledge in the cave. He pushed forward.

Ten feet.

Should he announce his arrival? Or was the Bigfoot nearby?

Five feet.

Paul crouched. Then called out softly, "Deidre?"

The humming stopped. There was a sudden movement in the light. Shadows moved and changed as Deidre moved around it. Perhaps she was trying to hide the things she'd taken.

"Deidre, it's me. Paul. I'm not upset. I know you were hungry. Let's get out of this place, go home."

Silence.

The light became brighter. A thin, white arm stuck out from the ledge—more of a stone room really, Paul could see now—and held a lantern before it. The rest of the figure's body was nothing more than an outline. He threw an arm over his eyes. The soft glow was blinding after so many hours in the darkness.

"Paul?" a voice cried. "Paul, is that really you?" He heard the lantern clatter and then looked up to see it fall sideways onto a stone nearby. A white hand shot out and righted it, and then the figure—the woman—hurled herself toward him.

"Paul! Paul!" She sobbed, scrambling down stones, half slipping and half running toward him.

"I—" he stood, immobile. This couldn't be real. He was having a hallucination.

Jane.

It was Jane who reached him and pulled him into her arms. Jane—his Jane—who peppered his face with kisses and then wrapped her arms around his neck.

Paul couldn't make out anything she was saying. She was crying and laughing and trying to talk all at the same time. Her words were so rushed and pushed together that he couldn't understand full sentences, just phrases: "here you are...wouldn't leave...so scared...never thought...oh, God, I can't believe..." He pressed her against him, holding her tightly, burying his face in her neck. She trembled hard against him and he could feel her heartbeat against his chest, fast and quick like bird wings.

They stood like that for a long, long time. Paul had so many questions. But Jane needed time. Time to process his appearance. Time to get her thoughts together. Time to talk after so many weeks with no one to talk to...

Finally, he pushed her back from his chest, just enough to look into her face. It was covered in tears that had made tracks over her dusty cheeks.

"I can't believe it. I just can't believe you did it, Jane. How have you survived here for so long?"

She kissed him again and when she drew back, laughed shakily. "Oh, Paul. I have so much to tell you. I can't believe you're here. Really here." She hugged him again, her mouth soft and hot on his. He could taste her tears now as he kissed her back. He was afraid he'd bruised her lips. Her clothing was rough under his hands, her stomach hard.

They held each other again for several long minutes. Finally, Jane said, "Come with me," and led him back toward the ledge. She guided him up, showed him with the light a way to place his feet so that he could scale the wall with a minimal amount of effort.

At the top was a sort of room. It was large and—Paul could hardly believe this—almost cozy. A pile of reeds had been woven and lay on the floor like a mat. On top of that was placed a blanket, similar to the one that Paul himself had carried, but a different color and, upon closer inspection, more threadbare. A small fire was burning in the corner of the room, a sliver of daylight visible above it where the smoke drifted up. There were cups and bowls made crudely out of stone. These sat on another, larger stone that was shaped like a table. In the corner was a stick from which hung a small, tattered photo of himself and Jane.

"What..." his voice trailed off as he looked around. "You did all of this?"

"Some of it. Some was already here," Jane said with a smile. She pulled his hand, leading him to the small woven mat. They sat on it, facing each other. Jane's eyes traveled over his face, his chest, his arms, then back up again.

"I can't believe it's you!" She put a hand on his cheek. Her fingers were rough and calloused. He pulled it free and kissed her palm, then held it gently in his lap.

"Please, tell me what happened," he said.

"Where should I start? The beginning, of course, I'll start there."

Paul nodded. No more words would come now, not if he tried.

Jane shifted slightly on the mat, her hand still clutching his as though she were afraid of breaking contact. As though he might disappear if she did.

"What do you remember last?" she asked.

Paul's brow furrowed. He'd tried so hard to forget those awful days, to push them down that it was difficult now to recall them.

"I remember...Allan."

Jane nodded solemnly.

"I remember my leg—the accident. After that though, things are pretty blurred. I had an infection they said at the hospital. I was delirious." He shook his head. The memories were like a kaleidoscope: fragments and bits that spun but with long spaces of blankness between.

"How did I get there? To the hospital when you and Deidre were left here?"

"I'll explain everything," Jane squeezed his hand. "Just try and keep an open mind."

*An open mind?* Paul nodded, wondering what she meant.

Jane took a deep breath, looked off toward the opening of the little stone room. He could see her trying to collect herself, organize her thoughts. Jane was always thorough and practical. She wouldn't use fifty words when ten would suffice. Finally, she turned back to Paul, smiled a little.

"After Deidre ran off and you were hurt, I was desperate for help. I left you twice to go out and try to find the trail again, see if I could find another hiker or a hunter passing through. The second time..." Jane's voice faltered. "After the second time, I knew I couldn't leave you again." She put a hand over her mouth, her eyes bright.

He touched her shoulder. "Hey, what is it? What happened?"

She shook her head, then cleared her throat. "Do you remember the symbols in the cave ceiling? Where we'd set up camp that night?"

Paul nodded.

"I think," Jane paused, shook her head. "No. I believe that they are tied to a spirit—a dark spirit—here. I call it the Shadow." Jane rushed on as though waiting for Paul to interrupt, call her foolish. He didn't know what to say so simply nodded again.

"Something evil lives in this cave. It acts like a disease, infiltrating the mind and then eating away at it. Makes its host do awful things. Things they'd never do in their right state. I think...I think it's tied to those symbols. The ones we saw." Jane shivered, looked toward the opening of the ledge. "When I came back that second time, you were delirious. At least, that's what I thought at first."

"At first."

Jane nodded. "But then I realized that it was the Shadow. It seems to prey on people in a weakened state." She stopped for a moment, looked away from him and toward the fire. "Paul, I know this must sound crazy, that you must think I'm insane. But it's true. I can't explain it all—not right now, maybe not ever—but I think it was trying to get inside you. Trying to take you over in a way. Control you."

Paul felt his heart thudding harder in his chest. He'd heard stories about what happened to people when they were alone too long. Jane had been out here—alone—for two months. What could happen to a person's mind when they were in a solitary state for that long?

Her eyes searched his face. They were as clear and intelligent as they'd always been. And Paul thought of the black fog and the voice he'd heard himself.

"I believe you," he said.

Jane smiled, relief apparent on her face.

"But you were saying something else. About not leaving me in the cave after the second time. What did you mean?"

"It..." Jane paused, bit her lip. "It was awful, Paul. I was so scared. You were saying things, things then that I know you wouldn't have otherwise."

"About what?"

"Not what. Who."

"Who then?"

Jane swallowed, glanced away. "Allan." Her voice was quiet. "You said ugly things about him. How you hated him, had always hated him. The way he flaunted money. The soft life he'd lived. That you were glad he was...were glad—he was dead," she said in a whisper. There was silence for a long moment, other than the distant roar of the brook and the occasional pop from the fire.

"You said that you hoped the same would happen to Deidre. That you wanted me to...to—"

"What?" Paul gripped Jane's arms suddenly, searching her face. "What did I want you to do?"

"To...die. No—you wanted to kill me." These last words came out in a rush. "I'd written a letter, describing what had happened here, to us. In case we didn't make it. And when I came back to the cave you'd...well. You'd written things. Terrible things."

Paul felt his hands slip down Jane's thin arms and hang loosely in his lap.

"It wasn't you, Paul." Jane's hands grasped his and squeezed. "I knew that. I knew it was the Shadow. I saw it—just once." She shivered suddenly and he felt her small hands vibrate slightly. "It was awful, terrifying. I knew then—just like now—that you'd never, ever do anything to hurt me. Not unless the Shadow could turn you somehow."

Paul released his wife's hands and let his head drop into his palms. Blood pounded in his ears, his face was hot with shame.

"Paul?" Jane sidled closer, put her hand through his arm, and tugged it gently. He couldn't look at her. Couldn't stand to see the kindness there. Guilt drove a sharp wedge into his heart.

"I'm sorry, Jane," his voice was little more than a hoarse whisper. "I'm so sorry."

"Oh, Paul, please don't," Jane said, her voice calm and clear. "There is no need to apologize. Not for something that wasn't your fault to begin with."

"What happened next?" Paul's voice was flat. Jane rubbed his arm with her hand, dropped a kiss on his shoulder. He couldn't feel the warmth of her lips through the thick material. He felt numb inside. Hollowed out.

"After...when I got back that time, I realized that it wasn't safe for you anymore in the cave. It wasn't safe for any of us. So, we started back toward the path. It was slow going—really slow—and I wasn't sure how long it would take us to get back down if we could even find the path.

"You were getting worse, your fever was, and you had become delirious. I didn't know what to do. I was so scared, Paul. All I could do was keep going forward. It looked like a storm was coming up and I thought I should go back, get our tent at least so we could stay dry. I was about to leave you, to go back to the cave for it...and that's when I saw it. Or I should say, I saw it again."

"What?"

"The—the creature—you remember that Deidre and I saw—it wasn't a bear, Paul. It was Bigfoot."

"I know. I saw it too."

Jane paused, surprised.

"You did?"

"I remember it—that night. I remember it standing over me. I remember its smell most—a musky, strange odor. And its eyes..." His voice trailed off. He closed his own eyes now, seeing the kaleidoscope images once more. This time they were varying shades of brown with intermittent glimpses of gold-colored eyes, matted hair, long arms...

Paul opened his eyes. "I tried to tell the doctor, the psychiatrist at the asylum, but he didn't believe me. It's why they put me there. Because I was talking about it. They thought I'd lost my mind up here."

"You didn't," Jane squeezed his arm again. "It's real. It's here, in this cave. In the woods."

"What?" Paul felt sweat along his hairline. "You've seen it since then?"

"It's good, Paul. It saved you on that day. It's saved me."

Paul's head felt as though he'd just finished an overly-fast ride on the merry-go-round at the county fair. His thoughts spun together and none of them made sense. The creature was good?

"Remember how I asked you to keep an open mind?"

Paul nodded mutely.

"It's not just the Shadow in this cave. That's evil. It seems to crave darkness. It feeds on negative emotions, on people's weaknesses and hurts. But the creature—the Bigfoot—is the opposite. It seems to be a sort of protector. It carried you back to the trail. I followed it. At first, I was scared, terrified that it would hurt you. But it didn't. It helped us, carried you back to Shiny Creek Trail. I followed it as far as that, but I had to go back. Had to try to find Deidre.

"How did you know that it wasn't carrying me off to my death? Or to its lair?"

Jane shrugged, a small smile on her face. "I could just tell. When you look at it—look right into its eyes—it communicates somehow. It doesn't speak but it can share its thoughts with you in other ways. Oh, I know this all sounds mad. But it's true."

Paul nodded. As Jane talked, he remembered the feeling of the creature standing over him. He remembered the sensation of being lifted—as though he were a baby or very small child—and being carried lightly. Gently.

"Do you think it brought me back to Allan's car?"

Jane nodded. "Or somewhere it knew other people would find you. I never saw anyone else on the trail after that day but I heard someone once. They'd gone by the time I found the trail again, but I discovered this blanket from where they'd made camp." She patted the woolen blanket on the mat.

"Why didn't you ever leave?"

She sighed. "I wanted to find Deidre, first. And bury Allan. It didn't seem right to just leave him hanging there..." her voice wobbled.

"But Deidre said she'd buried him."

"What?" Jane turned toward him, her eyes wide. "When did you see Deidre?"

"Just yesterday. Last night. She found me actually. I'd followed her footprints down at the brook. I thought they were yours. I spoke with her and—"

"Don't, Paul." Jane gripped his arm hard. "She's dangerous."

"What?" Paul sat back, feeling like someone had thrown a bucket of ice water over him. "What do you mean? She's starving, Jane. She looks close to death."

Jane's face grew dark. "Please. Promise me that if you see her again, you'll run."

Paul's wanted to laugh. He could see it now—him, a grown man running from the tiny, emaciated figure of Deidre.

"Have you seen her, Jane? Recently, I mean?"

Jane didn't answer. Instead, she stood, walked across the little room and added more branches to the fire. Her face was worried in the light from the flames, her brow creased, eyes narrowed.

Then Paul noticed something else. Jane's stomach was protruding abnormally, a swollen bump pushing against the fabric of her dress. He remembered photos he'd seen in *National Geographic* of starving children. The way their bellies poked out.

"Jane, are you...that is, have you found enough to eat? I'm sorry, I had food but it's...I lost it."

"I'm always hungry," she said, stirring the fire with a poker. "But I've found ways to survive." She turned to Paul, caught his gaze on her belly. Her face softened. "Paul, there's another reason that I didn't venture far from the cave. I've...I've been sick."

Guilt washed over Paul afresh. "I'm sorry, Jane."

"No, shhh, it's not like that." She moved across the space back to his side, knelt beside him. Then she took his hand and placed it on her stomach. "I certainly never imagined telling you quite like this. Paul, we're going to have a baby."

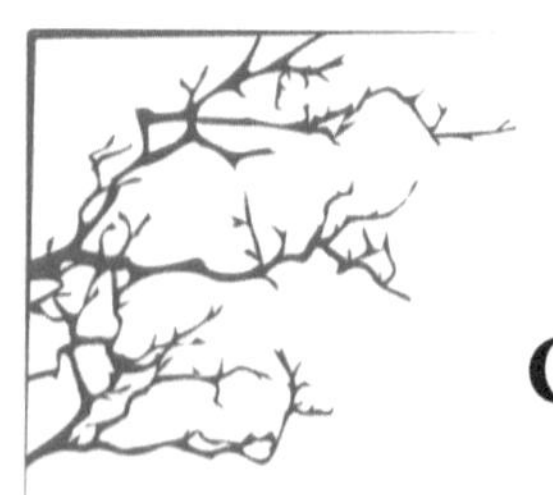

# Chapter Twelve

ALLAN WOKE WITH A START. He remembered two things immediately: the monster he'd seen in the darkness and that Deidre was gone. He shook his head slowly, tried to clear away the cobwebby stickiness in his mind.

The cave was quiet. Allan inventoried his body, testing hands, feet, legs, and arms, turning his neck and his head, which pounded. Then he let out a breath. A sense of hopelessness and despair pressed against him.

He'd failed.

*You are worthless.* The voice sidled up beside him, its whisper harsher, more grating than before.

Allan put his hands over his ears, then tried to get up. He stumbled, sank back down and tried again. The second time he made it, raised himself on spongy legs and leaned against a large boulder nearby.

*You couldn't even do the most simple of tasks. Punish her for what she did to you. She made you a laughing stock, Allan. You really are pitiful, aren't you?*

Allan felt the same shame from childhood, hot, sticky and sickening. He shook his head, tried to clear it. He'd had her here, right here in his arms. Had the knife...but then that beast had come out of nowhere, had tossed Allan as though he were a rag doll.

*It's because you're weak, Allan.* Again, the voice slithered through his mind. *So weak...* it trailed off, its whisper ending in a sigh. His parents had done that. Sighed over Allan. Never would he measure up to his golden sister, especially after her death. Then she and the baby were immortalized, living forever in a perfect memory in his parents' minds. Not to mention the minds of their family and friends...always there, a silent, accusing reminder of his inadequacy.

And then like a moving picture, Allan could see the past playing out behind his eyelids. Like Charlie Chaplin, the images danced across his mind. From childhood mistakes and disappointments to ways, he'd failed or disappointed or not been up to par as an adult. He heard the hushed voices when he entered a room; the pointed glances when he'd made a mistake in some new way; goals he'd set that had been thwarted. Allan could see the raised eyebrows and low murmurs about the "poor Warnings." And he felt the weight of it all like a physical pressure. It drove him to his knees. His head dropped into his hands, a sob rose in his throat.

*Why not end it all?*

The voice whispered, its voice loud—so loud—in Allan's ears. *Why not free yourself?*

He felt exhausted suddenly. So tired that it was an effort to even kneel. He shrank into himself, his body curling into a fetal position on the hard stones of the cave's floor.

*Worthless.* The voice hissed.

*Pathetic.*

Silence for a moment. Allan could hear the strange grating sound he'd heard earlier. It was closer now. Very close.

*You can stop the pain.*

Allan shook his head.

*You can be free, Allan.*

He stood again, leaned on the big boulder.

*Look.* The voice commanded and Allan knew he should look upward.

Above him, on the ceiling of the cave in a strange bluish light, he could see a stalactite—large and rough looking. Instead of the usual pointed tip, this one's edge curved up, back toward itself. Like a giant hook.

A sob rose in Allan's throat even as he found himself climbing the boulder. He stretched up. His fingers brushed the end of the formation. The tip of the hook. It was like it was meant to be here. For him.

*So easy to just let go...* the voice sighed. Allan felt himself nodding, his mind dull and his thoughts centered only on the voice and what it told him to do. He slipped his belt out of his trousers.

IT TOOK JANE MORE THAN two hours to find the cave again. When she did the fire had burned down to ashes. All of the supplies were still there, but the people weren't.

"Paul?" she called out. "Paul, are you there?"

The courage she'd felt in the other cave dissipated, leaving in its wake only a sick, pressing fear. She glanced up. The symbols were barely visible in the dim light, but she looked away, swallowed.

She needed to find Paul, find Deidre and Allan and tell them that they needed to leave—had to leave—right away.

But where was everyone?

Jane stood and listened for several long minutes. She heard the wind outside the cave's entrance and far away the sound of the underground brook. But here, in this part of the cave, there was nothing to suggest her husband or friends were nearby.

"Hello?" Jane called out. She moved further toward the back of the cave, where it began to taper and narrow. She hadn't been back there yet, didn't like enclosed spaces. It was darker here, harder to see. She went back to the packs, found a flashlight and tried again.

The light bounced off the rocks and stones, casting shadows that danced on the wall and underfoot. She kept the light as steady as she could, tried to take big, deep breaths.

*It's just a cave. There's no reason to be afraid.* She said the words over and over but fear squeezed her chest shut, making it hard to breathe.

A psalm came to mind, one her mother used to repeat every night before bed. "...though I walk through the valley and shadow of death, I will fear no evil. Your rod and staff, they comfort me..." Jane repeated the words over and over, casting the beam of light into the darkness and trying not to let her brain get stuck on the phrase, "shadow of death."

Then, she heard something. A mewling sound. Like a little kitten. There was a scraping noise too, like metal screeching against metal. It made the hair at the base of her neck stand up.

"Hello?" Jane said, her voice barely more than a whisper. "Paul? Deidre?"

No response.

Then there was a grunt, a whispered word—a plea?—it was hard to hear, too far away to make out. It was quiet then. She continued walking, repeating the verse over and over to herself.

Seconds later, Jane felt rather than saw something further ahead. A shifting in the dark shadows. A movement that was too far away to make out.

Or had she imagined it? She blinked, looked again.

There was nothing there.

She took another step then one more before she saw it again. A presence in the shadows. Something darker up above her moving against the grayness of the interior walls. She squatted low, flicked off the flashlight.

What was it? She wanted to cry out—call for her husband and her friends—but remained motionless. Then in one quick movement, before she could change her mind, she shone the light into the darkness. She cried out when she saw the scene illuminated in its beam.

Allan swung from the ceiling of the cave, his legs limp, his eyes bulging.

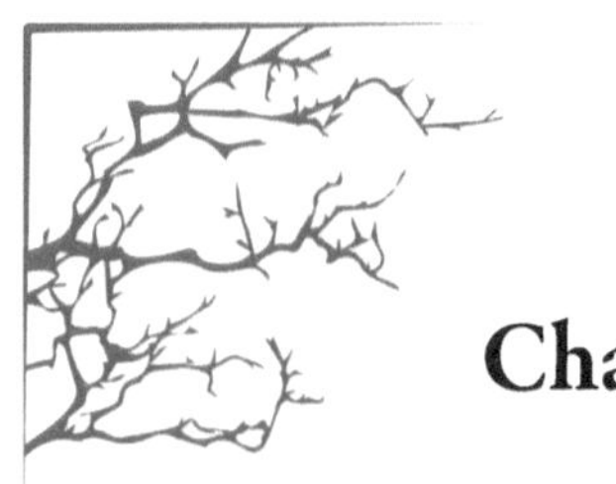

# Chapter Thirteen

"A...A BABY?" PAUL BREATHED the word as though it were hallowed. "You're pregnant?" Then, without waiting for an answer, "But when? How?"

Jane laughed. "Are you happy?"

Paul struggled to his feet and pulled Jane up with him. He hugged her hard, and with a whoop picked her up and swung her in one full circle. Then he quickly set her down. "I'm sorry. I will have to be more careful, now that...Jane. We're going to be...be parents?"

She smiled, nodded. "Yes. I knew before we came here, at least, I suspected. But I didn't want to be left behind. I've felt it kick, Paul."

"Have you?" Paul gingerly put a hand on Jane's belly. She placed her own over his. "How long? How long until he comes?" he asked.

"He?" Jane teased. "How do you know it's going to be a boy?"

Paul laughed. He couldn't remember the last time he'd done so. It felt good like something had broken loose inside.

"If I'm right, then I'm about five months along."

"Five months?" Paul breathed. In four months he'd be a father. A father. And Jane would be a mother. What a perfect role. He could see her already, baby nestled in her arms, her long hair over one shoulder, rocking and humming and kissing the top of a downy head.

"You are an amazing woman, Jane Rogers," Paul said, his voice low, husky. "You survived all these weeks not only taking care of yourself but a baby."

Jane shook her head. "It was because of the baby I survived. After you'd gone and Deidre... Well. When I was all alone, I couldn't just think about myself. I had another life—another person—depending on me. It helped get me through the hardest parts."

Paul couldn't stop grinning. But then he thought of what lay ahead of them and the smile faded.

"We need to go, to get out of here. We need to get you both back to civilization. After we find Deidre, we can all—"

"Paul," Jane said and put a hand on his arm. "There's something you need to know. About Deidre."

Paul looked at Jane. Her features were marred, sadness blurring the edges. "We can't save her. It's too late for that."

"But she seemed fine when I talked with her. She is painfully skinny of course, and will need rest, time to heal, but—"

"No." Jane's voice was firm. "She's lost."

"If you saw her, Jane. Maybe I could leave another note. I left one in the silt down by the brook for you—if we left another—"

"Paul! Listen to me." Jane's voice was loud and clear in the small space. "We have to leave her behind. She's been turned. By that thing—the Shadow—there's no way to save her now. We need to go—just us—and leave her here."

"But she's your friend. You love Deidre, Jane."

Jane paused and let out a shaky exhale. "I know. I did love her very much. Like a sister. But I love you and our baby more. We can't help her now. Not anymore."

Jane turned and walked over to the mat they'd been sitting on earlier. She flipped back a corner of it and withdrew a knife. The blade glinted in the light. "I sleep with this every night and I wear it every time I leave this place. She doesn't seem to come back here—she likes it by the entrance of the cave—near the symbols, I think. I saw her once by the brook but she didn't see me that day. Another time though...another time she attacked me. It was bad. I was terrified she'd kill me, hurt the baby."

"She didn't?"

"Just scratches and bruises. The creature—it protected me. Tossed her away from me and into the brook. It brought me here afterward. And since then I've been a lot more careful." Jane frowned, a furrow marring her otherwise smooth forehead. "I don't think that Deidre is quite human anymore, Paul. She's been turned into... Well. Something else."

Paul thought again of his conversation with Deidre. She'd seemed afraid, yes, and starving. But dangerous? And then he remembered her eyes. The hollow blankness that he'd written off to malnutrition and weeks of being alone. Being afraid. Had it been madness? Or like Jane said, something else?

"We should go," Jane said again. She gathered the knife, the lantern—where had she gotten oil for it? Paul wondered—and motioned to him. "I have a little food left," she pulled a packet of fabric from underneath the little table. "Rabbit meat." She tied it to her waistband. "It should last another day or two if we're careful."

Paul nodded. "I saw another tunnel a little ways back. It seemed to go to the outdoors."

"It does. That's how I go in and out when I need to. But we need to go to the brook first and fill ourselves with water. I don't have anything other than the jug," she pointed to the stone pitcher on the crude table. "And we can't carry that with us. But we should at least drink deeply, as much as we can. It might be a while before we find water again."

Paul grabbed his walking stick and eased back down the ledge as Jane held the light. As soon as they were on the cave's floor, she turned it off, left it hidden behind a pile of stones.

"I found it here, in this room," Jane answered his unasked question. "But I never use light in the cave," she whispered. She didn't offer more of an explanation and Paul didn't ask. It took several long seconds for his eyes to readjust to the darkness.

They began to walk. Jane led the way, her hand in Paul's. They traveled much more quickly than he had on his own. There was a sort of invisible path that Jane followed, trod many times he suspected in the past months. Their footsteps were nearly silent in the space. He could hear the same dripping of water off of rocks in faraway crevices, the muted hum from the underground brook, growing louder.

Jane stopped suddenly and Paul bumped into her.

"Sorry," he whispered close to her ear. "What is it?"

Jane shook her head slightly. "Shh," she whispered back. Then, "Listen."

Paul listened. He heard nothing out of the ordinary. "I don't hear any—" but then, as though an icy finger drew itself up his backbone, Paul felt a shiver roll down his body.

Far away, he could hear the strange grating sound that had become so familiar.

"It's the Shadow. Hurry," Jane said and pulled at his arm.

They moved faster then, over rocks and around boulders. At one point Paul thought that surely they were lost.

But Jane urged him on. "We're getting close." And then after a turn in the bend, he could hear the rushing water more clearly. They were indeed nearly there.

Jane was whispering something as they moved, the same few words over and over making a soothing cadence. But he couldn't make out what the words were.

"This way," Jane said and tugged him toward the edge of the ravine. It was lighter here, by some miracle and they climbed carefully down over the rocks. They were slippery under Paul's hands and feet. The air here was laced with a strange mixture of loamy dankness and fresh vapor from the rushing water. The brook undulated in the dim light. He wished he could turn on a flashlight or that they could have brought the lantern. What animals lived here? Raccoons? Mountain lions? Bear? Paul shivered involuntarily.

"There's a good spot down here," Jane whispered loudly, close to Paul's face as she tugged on his hand. "The water is calmer and easier to get to."

Paul followed his wife but kept his eyes and ears tuned to the rocks and boulders and stones around him. His other hand clutched his walking stick. At least he'd managed to keep it if nothing else.

He thought suddenly of their little apartment. It was the third story on Main Street in downtown Burlington. Close to the theater, restaurants, and jazz clubs. He thought of how they'd typically spend their weekends: the long, slow mornings in bed on Saturday, then wandering around the market. Working on a story while Jane read in the chair nearby in the afternoon and then dinner out—sometimes with friends, sometimes just the two of them—and relaxing in bed after a long day. Paul wanted that now. The security, the knowingness of what was coming next, what to expect. He craved it suddenly like physical hunger. He had to keep them safe, get them back to their real life. Their ordinary, everyday—

"Here, Paul," Jane said and tugged him down toward the water. He followed her, finding a small indent in the rocks where she positioned herself. "You keep watch while I drink. Then I'll do the same for you."

Paul nodded, then realized that Jane couldn't see him in the dim light. "Sure."

He scanned the rocks and boulders behind them, looking for any movement, any change in the shadows. At first, he heard only the same sounds that had become the backdrop of this place. But moments later, Paul heard something else. Something out of place. The sound of rocks clinked together behind and to his right. He whirled around, his staff raised. A muskrat skittered over some wet stones and splashed into the water.

He laughed weakly. Jane was kneeling on the bank, her face to the water, drinking. He could just make out the white half-moon of her face in the pale light. How much water could their bellies hold? And how long would it sustain them? If only he had the canteen! If only—

"Your turn," Jane said over her shoulder. Paul reached for her, helped her to her feet. Her face sparkled with water droplets. She wiped a hand over it and motioned to the water. "I'll keep watch," she said and held out a hand for his walking stick.

Paul hadn't realized how thirsty he was until he started drinking. The water was icy cold, numbing his mouth and causing an instant soreness in his forehead. But he kept drinking until his stomach started to feel nauseous. Then he pulled away, glanced over his shoulder.

Jane was standing there, behind him. But something wasn't right. His smile slid off his face as he took in her strange position. Her feet were askew, as though she wasn't really standing on them at all. As though she was a puppet. He glanced upward. Jane's face was a mask of fear, her mouth pulled wide, terror in her eyes.

"Thought you might come here," she said.

No, Paul realized. It was a female voice and was coming from Jane's direction. But it wasn't Jane.

It was Deidre's.

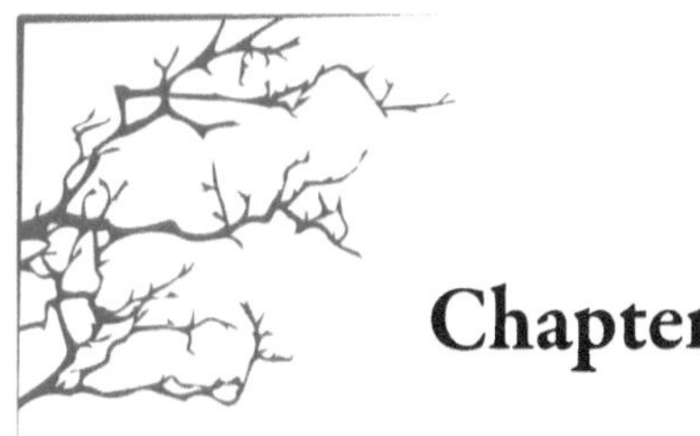

# Chapter Fourteen

*Jane Rogers*
*Saturday, September 8, 1917*
*Shiny Creek Trail*

JANE'S SCREAMS RICOCHETED off the cave walls. It became like a living thing, twisting and wrapping itself around rocks and boulders. Her throat was raw and hot. And then when the cry ended, she clamped a hand over her mouth. As though she was trying to keep the rest in.

She couldn't look away from the body swinging above her. Like coming across a house fire or an automobile accident, her eyes were drawn there against her will.

There was a jagged, hook-like rock—or maybe stalactite?—slightly to the left of Allan. He'd wound his belt around his neck and the hook and then must have stepped off the boulder.

His face was contorted in the shadows, as though he were surprised by the pain in the end. Had he been? Had he died right away or slowly strangled? Jane felt hot, wet tracks down her face. She realized then that she was rocking a little on her feet. A quiet moan like a dull hum came from the back of her throat.

Where was Deidre? Had she seen her husband?

Another thought butted these out of the way. Where was Paul? Was he dead too?

A panicked burst of terror flew up Jane's throat. She began trembling all over, her limbs shaking. She put a hand out to steady herself on the boulder, then stopped, and stepped back. Below her, something glinted. She knelt slowly. It was a knife. Its blade was dark and sticky, its handle satiny under her fingertips when she picked it up. The blade looked ferociously sharp. Jane didn't recognize it. Perhaps it had been Allan's? She didn't allow her gaze to refocus on the body above her. *Don't do it. Don't look. You must find Paul. Find Deidre. Get away from here. Get help.*

She stumbled forward, holding the knife out in front of her like a flashlight. Where was her flashlight? She frowned suddenly. She'd been holding it. It must have fallen. She glanced around the floor of the cave and then realized that stupidly, she'd dropped it. It was wedged in a tight split between two medium-sized rocks. The light was still on, shining toward the ground and she put her hand out and pulled.

It was stuck, wedged tightly between the two stones. She placed the knife carefully on a nearby stone and used both hands on the smooth flashlight. Her hands felt greasy. Coated with sweat or dampness from the cave, she wasn't sure which. They slipped and slid from the cylindrical shape again and again.

A noise sounded behind her. Branches snapped in the far side of the cave. Feet hurried quickly over stones. Jane grabbed the knife and turned. She swung it out in front of her, brandishing it at the dark figure moving toward her.

"Jane?" the voice called.

Jane's breath came out in a whoosh.

"Paul." Her voice was shaky and timid sounding. "Oh, Paul."

He reached her just as she crumpled. She dropped the knife and fell into his chest, feeling his strong arms wrap around her. She was crying again, she realized, as though she were experiencing someone else's body. Her tears soaked through Paul's vest.

"Jane, what's the matter? I looked all over for you and couldn't—"

"He's dead," she said the words so quietly she barely heard them.

"Allan?" his voice broke slightly. "When? How?"

"He's...up there."

Jane motioned to the shadowy form above them. Paul's body stiffened. She felt him swallow, felt his Adam's apple bob against the side of her head. A strangled sound came from his throat.

"My God." His voice didn't sound like his voice. "We have to get him down, Jane. I've got to help him."

Before she could say anything, Paul was already clambering up the steep boulder.

"Don't, Paul. It's too late!"

He ignored her or didn't hear her. She watched, her fingernails jammed into her palms as he balanced precariously on the boulder. It was damp—everything was damp—and his feet couldn't find purchase there.

"Paul! Paul, be careful. Please be careful."

Finally, he made it the rest of the way up the boulder. He positioned himself under his friend's legs and lifted upward, trying to loosen the makeshift noose around Allan's neck.

"Paul, it's too late," Jane said again, hating herself a little. Still, it was true. And what if something happened to Paul, trying to get Allan's body down?

"Jane, I need something sharp—where's your jackknife?"

Jackknife? Jane tried to think. She couldn't even remember where her pack was. Then, "Here," she said, stooping to again retrieve the knife. She handed it gingerly to Paul, handle out. He released his hold just slightly on Allan's legs to take it from her. Then he stretched, reaching as high as he could. The knife blade was too short. Just centimeters though, an inch at the most. If he could stretch just a little higher...

Instead, Paul's right foot slid down the slippery face of the boulder. It threw his entire body off balance and his legs started to veer in opposite directions. He tried to correct his balance. Tried to move himself and counteract his weight. Instead, with a yell, he slipped from the boulder. Allan swung once again, dangling and twisting at the end of the noose. Jane watched, horrified, as Paul tipped forward. He flailed his arms and then, as though in slow motion fell back and disappeared over the backside of the boulder.

Jane screamed. Then she scrambled around the smaller rocks to get to Paul. He'd had the knife in his hand as he'd fallen. *Please, God. Please let him have let go of it.*

She scrambled over the wet stones, slipping and scraping off the skin on her hands and shins.

"Paul!" she shouted. "Paul!"

When she reached the other side of the boulder, she could see his body. It looked crumpled, like a doll that had collapsed in on itself after a child had thrown it down. It was darker here, without the light but she didn't immediately see blood or the knife anywhere.

"Paul?" Her voice bounced over the rocks nearby. "Paul, are you all right?"

He moaned in response. She frantically scrabbled over the last few large stones to his side.

"My leg," he said, his face a grimace of pain. "Can you help me up?" His breath came in tight little bursts.

Jane squatted near his shoulders and wrapped her arms underneath them. Then carefully, slowly, she helped him up. Leaving him propped against the boulder, Jane rushed back and managed to get the flashlight, then hurriedly retraced her steps.

Paul's leg didn't look good. The pant leg of his right leg was torn open and underneath the skin was gone. In its place was a wide swath of bloody, oozing flesh. He put weight on the leg gingerly and gave a yell.

"I must have sprained my ankle," he said. "Or broken it."

Blood flowed in rivulets down his calf, over his boot, and pooled underneath his foot. Jane ripped the sleeves from her blouse and tied them together.

"We have to get this bleeding to stop," she said, crouching. "I'm sorry. This is probably going to be uncomfortable."

Paul only grunted in response. He looked away as she wound the material snugly over his shin. Part of the fabric instantly bloomed red.

"It's just a surface abrasion," she said although she wasn't sure at all that's all it was. "But we still need to keep it clean, stop the bleeding. We can create a splint for your ankle back at camp." Paul's breath was becoming labored as she stood and wrapped his arm over her shoulders. "Come on. Lean on me." He did so, his breath warm in her hair.

"I'm sorry, Jane," he said. "What a stupid thing to do."

"You were trying to help a friend," she said quietly. "It was a noble attempt."

Paul made a strangled laughing sound in his throat. "I don't think noble quite describes it. More like clumsy."

It took them a long time to get back to camp. On flat ground, it would have been easier and less painful for Paul. Here, they had to stop every few feet and readjust Paul's position. Let him rest his injured leg.

Finally, they made it back to the entrance of the cave. The fire had burned out, the space was cold and dark. Jane helped Paul lower himself to his bedroll. Then, with shaking fingers she rebuilt the fire and started a pot of water heating.

"I need to go back and get something," Jane said. Paul's eyes were shutting. They fluttered at her voice. Was that a sign of shock? She hoped not.

"Be careful," he whispered.

"I will," she said. Then she turned and headed back into the darkness. She had to get the flashlight and the knife. They would need every single supply they had now.

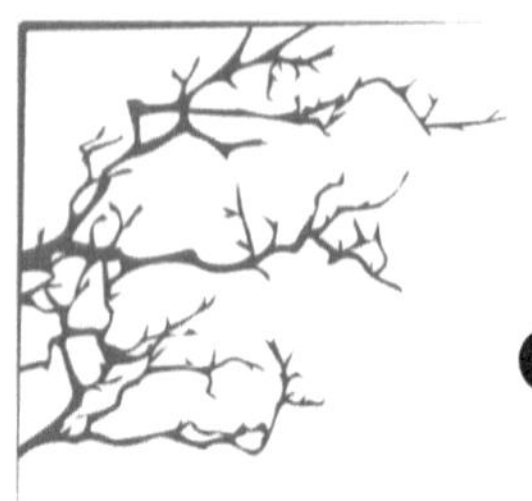

# Chapter Fifteen



*Paul Rogers*
*Sunday, November 11, 1917*
*Shiny Creek Trail*

PAUL COULD SEE THE skeletal fingers digging so hard into the flesh of Jane's neck that thin lines of blood trickled down into her collar. Deidre's tiny frame was hidden behind Jane's. She'd grabbed Jane's right arm and wrenched it behind her back and Jane's body bucked and jerked as the arm was twisted forcefully. Jane cried out.

Deidre's pale face was barely visible over Jane's shoulder. Her eyes were little more than dark holes in her skull that stared out at him. Her face was twisted and ugly. Then Paul saw something that made his heart jerk hard in his chest before it galloped on. Oozing from the sleeves of Deidre's tattered blouse were tendrils of black mist. He stared in horror. The mist seemed to follow her movements or control them, he couldn't tell which. As she moved her hand slightly, the black fog rolled from her sleeves and close to Jane.

Paul lunged toward them. He had to free Jane.

Deidre anticipated his movement and jerked his wife backward. Jane stumbled, catching her foot on a rock, and cried out as Deidre tightened her grip on Jane's arm. Paul stopped moving. The two women swayed slightly on their feet as though the wind blew hard against them.

"That's right, Paul. Better to listen to me than try any heroics." Deidre's voice creaked loudly in the space like a rusted hinge scraping against a doorframe. Her voice was so different, so mechanical than it had been when they'd sat by the fire. More of the black smoke spilled from her mouth as she spoke.

Paul dragged his eyes to Jane's face. She was grimacing in pain, her lips pressed together hard between her teeth. She looked toward the water, the brook. She was trying to tell him something, but what? He wished he'd insisted on carrying the knife. Wished he'd paid more attention as he drank from the brook. Wished he had a gun.

Deidre's voice made a horrible sound and it took Paul a minute to realize that she was laughing. It sounded inhuman. Like an animal in a trap or a woman being strangled. The sound bounced off rocks and stones.

Her next words cut him to the core. "Poor Jane," she cooed, moving her face inches from his wife's. "You came so far and survived so much. Only to be killed by your best friend. I am still your best friend, aren't I, Jane?" the mechanical-sounding laughter started again.

Jane caught Paul's eye and moved her own to the left, toward the water again. What did she want Paul to do? Find a stone and clobber Deidre? Make a run for it? He shook his head slightly.

"Poor, poor stupid Paul," Deidre said. "You really are worthless, you know that? Completely worthless." The last word came out as a hiss. Jane's eyes filled with tears as Deidre jerked her back again. Rivulets of blood ran freely down Jane's neck now. He could see her trying to swallow, trying to take a breath. Deidre was choking her. With skeletal-like fingers that seemed inhumanly long, she dug into the tender white skin of Jane's neck, squeezing and squeezing.

"You both thought you could leave me here. Leave me to rot in this place. It will be you who dies here, Jane." She jerked Jane's neck a little and Jane gasped in pain. "And then I'll kill Paul."

A cold sweat broke out on Paul's skin. He motioned to Deidre to stop. "Please, Deidre. Let her go. It's me you want, isn't it? I'm the one who failed you. Failed you both. I should have come back with help right away. I was—I was weak." He took a step toward the women. "You wouldn't have suffered this way if it wasn't for me."

Deidre paused in her awkward backward shuffle. She must have loosened the pressure slightly on Jane's neck because he could hear Jane pulling halting, jerky breaths of air into her lungs.

"Oh, I'll take care of you too, Paul. But afterward." Deidre craned her neck so she could look at Jane's face. She put her own next to it, whispered something in Jane's ear. Jane closed her eyes, her lips trembled.

Paul saw his chance. He rushed toward the brook, away from Deidre and Jane. He ran through the water. The iciness of it made his legs numb within seconds. He stumbled, lurched, nearly fell as his foot hit a slippery rock but then righted himself. Deidre screamed something at him. He pushed onward, sharp daggers of cold soaking his legs, arms, and even some of his torso.

*Please, God. Please, if you're real, save Jane.*

Would Deidre come after him? Had he guessed right, that she wanted an audience? His breath was coming hard in his chest. Not from exertion—not yet—but the adrenaline streaming through his system.

He heard a noise behind him then. Feet slapping over rocks. Scrabbling sounds as Deidre scaled the stones and boulders along the shore. How could she move so quickly? Paul chanced a glance over his shoulder and stumbled again. She was on all fours. Running over the rocks and boulders like a beast. Like a cat. She leaped from one to the next, her hair hanging in her face, then flying backward as she leaped to the next rock. Her lips were pulled back into a grimace. Thin tendrils of black fog streamed out behind her.

Paul tripped and fell. His right knee connected hard with a stone. Pain radiated down to the site of his old injury. Deidre was nearby now, on a large boulder. She crouched. He groaned and tried to get up. Frigid water splashed as he struggled to right himself.

"Oh dear, Paul. What a shame," Deidre giggled. The sound was a sickening mixture of girlish delight and demonic hiss. "Let me help."

Paul turned, tried to run deeper into the brook. Where? Could he make it across to the other side? But then, what about Jane? He plunged his hands into the water, picked up the first medium-sized stone he could find. He hurled it toward Deidre. She easily moved out of the way and it cracked against a boulder and tumbled somewhere in the dark.

He lunged toward her but made it only two agonizing steps before he felt Deidre's fingers spread like talons around his neck. She lifted him up—out of the brook—and plunged him down again. He tried to break his fall. Put his arms out, tried to yell. But the frigid water closed over him. Everything was muffled and loud simultaneously. His instinct was to draw his breath in, the water so cold it made him gasp, and when he did he started to choke and thrash. Deidre pulled him effortlessly from the water then. She was giggling again as she dragged him onto the shore. He couldn't feel his arms or legs. Everything was numb with cold.

The silt beneath him was sticky and pulled at his boots. He struggled to stay upright, keep his footing. Fiery tracks of pain lacerated his neck. She'd switched positions, standing behind him now. Paul looked around blearily. Where was Jane? Had she gotten away? He jerked his hands to where Deidre's fingers dug into his neck. But as he did she snagged one arm just as she had Jane's. Deidre jerked it so hard behind his back that stars burst before Paul's eyes. Her strength was incredible—superhuman—and he grunted, trying hard to keep from shouting in pain.

She dragged him toward a tall boulder nearby. Her breath was hot and rancid on his face. He struggled, trying to use his free arm to grab her—any part of her—and get a hold. Above the dull thrum of the water over stones, he could hear the same grating, scratching sounds he had earlier. He tried to look behind him but she jerked harder on his other arm. So hard that something popped in his shoulder. Fireworks of blue pain exploded. Paul cried out. Deidre dropped that arm which hung uselessly at his side. Fire roared through his shoulder. She had dislocated it.

Deidre kept her grip on the back of his neck. He could feel trickles of warmth dripping down and pooling in his collarbone. He swung out with his good arm behind him, trying and failing to grab her skin, her clothes. Deidre grabbed this arm and wrenched it behind him.

"Stupid fool." She laughed again, her voice reminiscent of the Deidre he'd always known—teasing and flirtatious. "Don't fight me, Paul. I'm much too powerful. Do you know what it's been like for me here?

"You deserted me—all of you—left me behind to die. First Allan—poor, weak Allan—and then you." She tightened her grip on his neck. Paul could feel his eyes bulging. He thought of a little chipmunk he'd tried to rescue as a boy—it had been run over by the wheels of a wagon. Its eyes had bulged so far out of its head that Paul had stared—half in fascination, half in horror—at it before creating a little nest for it in an old cookie tin. He felt like that now. Helpless. At the mercy of someone—or something?— more powerful than himself. He closed his eyes, focusing all his strength and energy on drawing his next breath.

"What's the matter, Paul," Deidre crooned. His eyes flew open as she moved her mouth to his ear. "Are you scared?" She chuckled and a cloud of foul breath covered his face. It was colored, her breath, an inky black. "You should be." Her voice had turned into a growl. With a single hand wrapped around his neck, she lifted him from the cave floor. He dangled above it as she maneuvered her way to the top of the nearby boulder. She was panting hard. Paul willed his lifeless arm to do something but it dangled uselessly at his side. He bent forward, trying to free his other arm from her grasp. Instead, she simply tightened it—he didn't think that was possible—and he let out a choking yell as burning heat raced up his arm and shoulder.

"Don't worry, Paul. It will all be over soon. Then I'll help Jane."

"Don't...you—" his voice was barely more than a pain-filled whisper, "—touch her."

He looked over his shoulder at her face as she started to respond. Searching for a sign—any sign—that some of her humanity remained. But her black eyes glittered back at him and the expression she wore was flat and blank like a death mask. When her lips stretched wide over her teeth, tendrils of black mist swirled out of the sides of her lips. She raised him with one hand. Paul dangled like a puppet over the ground below. Beneath the boulder, they stood on was a crevasse between some smaller rocks. Twenty feet down? Thirty? She was going to throw him there. He could feel it already—the pain shooting like darts all over his body, the explosive heat ripping through his limbs. He wanted to yell, to fight her, to do something—but he was impotent in her grip.

Then Paul heard a sound like a freight train filling the space. It drowned out the sound of the brook, the sound of Deidre's harsh breath. It shook the stones under their feet. Deidre's grip slipped slightly on the back of his neck and his arm. He took advantage of it and pitched himself backward. She scrabbled to get a better hold of him.

For a few seconds, time stopped. Paul felt, rather than saw the figure towering over them. On a nearby boulder, the creature stood. Its arms too long, its hair matted. Paul smelled the same musky scent that he remembered from months ago. Both of their heads turned toward the beast—his and Deidre's—and then he heard her cry out a single word, "No!"

The beast reached forward in one graceful motion and clasped Deidre around the waist. It jerked her and Paul apart. Paul felt himself pitch forward and caught himself on the boulder inches before sliding off. Deidre screamed and beat her hands against the creature. It lifted her close to its face. Its eyes—like liquid gold—studied her. She quieted for a moment as though mesmerized. Then it roared that freight-train roar again directly into her face. Paul ducked his head, covering one side with his good shoulder and shutting his eyes instinctively.

He heard her fall. Heard her exclamation of surprise turn into a scream of terror. When he opened his eyes again, Deidre's body lay in the crevasse beneath him. She was prone at an odd angle. Her ribs jutted forward on one side, broken. Some poked through her blouse. A dark pool of blood covered the rock where her head lay. Her right leg was turned unnaturally and one of her boots dangled precariously from her twisted foot. Her face looked upward in surprise toward Paul.

There was no light in her eyes.

Paul lay on his side on the boulder, gasping for breath as his eyes darted around for the creature. There! From the corner of his eye, Paul saw movement in the shadows. But Jane, not the man-beast, appeared. She walked unsteadily, supporting herself on the rocks and boulders.

"Paul?" her voice was hesitant and scared. "Paul?" Her right hand was covering her belly.

"Jane," he said, his voice a whisper. He rolled over, letting momentum pull his body down the face of the boulder. He half-fell and half-climbed the rest of the way to the floor of the cave.

"I'm here, Jane. I'm here. It's all right." His voice was a choking croak that made him cough. He stumbled toward her.

They met halfway, her arms and his good one tangling around each other. Their bodies were both shaking. Paul wasn't sure which of them was holding the other up. He kissed her head once, twice.

"It's all right now," he said. "It's all right. Let's go, Jane." And he led her away from the sight of Deidre's crumpled body in the rocks.

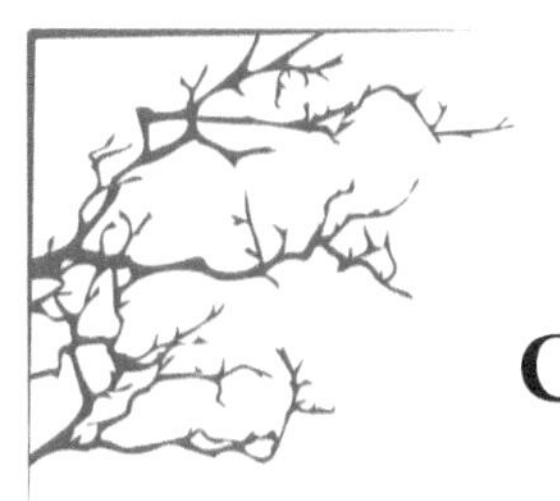

# Chapter Sixteen

*Jane Rogers*
*Sunday, September 9, 1917*
*Shiny Creek Trail*

DAWN BROKE EARLY AND Jane watched it happen. She'd barely slept during the night. The wind shrieked around the edges of the cave. The storm that had missed them on their first day in the woods had circled back around.

Rain pelted hard on the rocks and trees outside the cave's entrance. The wind tore at the leaves, carrying gusts of debris past. Branches and grasses rolled like tumbleweeds before getting tangled in bushes and vegetation. Occasionally, the branches were hurled to the ground and landed with a crack, making Jane jump.

Paul slept, blissfully unaware of his surroundings. Jane scooted closer to her husband, reaching down to flip up his blanket again and look at the wound. It had stopped bleeding, finally. They'd created a temporary split from straight branches and strips of cloth Jane had torn from the skirt in her pack. She'd put what was left of it back on along with a jacket she had packed, grateful for the extra warmth. Still, she shivered as she poked at the small fire. Sparks rose upward toward the ceiling.

"They're kind of beautiful, aren't they?"

Paul's voice startled her. She looked at him. He was still flat on his back, only now his eyes were opened, staring at the symbols on the ceiling.

"Are they?" Her voice was tight. Looking at them made a prickle of dread crawl up her back. She shifted. "A storm has come in."

"Mmm," Paul said, his eyes unblinking. "I think they're trying to tell a story. Don't you?"

"Paul," Jane said, her voice firm. "You said yourself the first night that they weren't civilized. I don't like them. They look—I don't know—demonic. Anyway, I think we should discuss our next steps." Could he tell she was only pretending confidence? "How we're going to get out of here."

Paul ignored her. She watched as his eyes tracked the circle of marks above.

"Paul," she said again and gave his good leg a little shake. He frowned, glanced at her. His eyes...they were strange. Unfocused. As though he were looking through her, not at her. She moved closer to the head of his bedroll, placed a hand on his forehead. It was cool and dry, not feverish as she'd expected. She held the canteen up to his mouth. Her hand trembled a little.

"We need to go—get help for...for Allan. And find Deidre. I'd hoped she might come back here tonight, but I haven't seen or heard her. I hope she's somewhere safe. Out of the wind and the rain—"

"Allan was a greedy bastard." Paul interrupted. "He deserved what he got." His voice was strange and slow. It caused goosebumps to run up and down Jane's arms and legs. She was so shocked she couldn't speak.

"What?" she finally blurted out. "What are you talking about? He was your best friend."

Paul shook his head. "He always liked to lord it over me, you know. His family's wealth. His position in the world. Constantly had to rub it in that he had the better car, a better apartment, and he could afford the better entertainment. You know what I mean, don't you, Jane? Just last weekend at the restaurant."

Paul's words were jumbled like he was struggling to make the syllables flow in the right way. Jane stared at him.

But she did know what he meant. The beautiful meal at *Mon Petit* was marred by Allan's insistence that they all enjoy the most expensive bottle of wine the venue offered. Generous, one would think. Until realizing that it was only to trump the lower-end bottle that Paul had already purchased, which Allan had sent back after taking a single sip.

"Like motor oil, friend," he'd laughed, clapping Paul on the back. Then he'd turned to the waiter hovering at his shoulder. "Bring me your best and oldest bottle. I spare no expense where my friends are concerned."

Implying of course, that Paul did.

Both men made a similar salary at the newspaper. But Allan's family and their connections put him worlds' ahead of Paul in their other publishing ventures. While Allan had been published last year in *LIFE* magazine, Paul was still scrabbling to find placement for his "pet projects," as Allan called them, in journals outside the New England area.

Jane swallowed. It was one of the reasons that this trip had been so important. It was going to be the story of a lifetime. One that would set both Allan and Paul apart, and hopefully in Paul's case, launch his writing career to a new level.

Except, it hadn't turned out that way.

"You don't mean that, Paul," Jane said, her voice quiet. "He was your best friend. You've defended him to others more times than I can count. You said yourself that even if he was born with a silver spoon, he figured out how to eat with his own hand."

Paul laughed, a choked, angry sound. "Ah yes. It's easy to use your hand when your father is propping it up. And Deidre. She—"

"Stop. Stop it, Paul. You're not yourself." Heat flooded Jane's cheeks. "This isn't you talking."

He didn't respond. When Jane glanced over at him, his eyes were half-closed and focused once more on the ceiling.

"I'm going to pack things up now." Jane's voice was clear as she started stuffing things randomly into their packs. "Then we'll heat water for coffee and eat and be on our way. Oh, and I'll look for a branch that we might fashion into a crutch for you, too. I—"

But Paul had fallen asleep, or at least closed his eyes and pretended to. Jane pressed her palms against her eyes.

*He didn't mean it. He didn't mean it. He didn't mean it.*

Still, the ugly words hung in the air above their heads, swirling and undulating as though a physical presence.

Jane pulled the little coffee pot from her pack and set it over the fire, filling it with water. She'd start heating the water before she went out to find a good makeshift crutch. She looked in the pack again, trying to find their tin cups. Instead, her fingers closed over a notebook and pen. As she opened the pad of paper two other pieces of paper fluttered gently to the cave's floor. The articles. The ones that had inspired their trip here.

She smoothed her fingers over the first.

*Man Missing on Shiny Creek Trail*

*Mister James Smithfield, 18 years of age, was reported missing on Tuesday, the seventh of July, 1897. Mister Smithfield was last seen by a group of friends on the Shiny Creek trail in Little River. The group left for a two-day hike, which was supposed to convene at Shiny Creek on Wednesday, the eighth of July. However, Mister Smith was last seen entering the woods near the camp that the group had created. He was not seen after this time.*

*A fellow member of the hiking group and friend, Mister James Winters, stated that he had, "seen a monster," in the woods near the trail where Mister Smithfield was last seen. The area was searched by state officials and there were no signs of foul play. Anyone with details or information to share with authorities is encouraged to contact the local police department.*

Jane set the clipping aside and pulled out the second.

*Beast Seen on Trail in Little River*

*Three hunters found a creature they were not bargaining for when they entered the woods on the fifteenth of October. While the men were hunting grouse and deer, one man, Mister Daniel Elkhorn, took a photograph of this suspicious-looking animal. "It was a man-beast," said Elkhorn, who was undeniably shaken after the event. "I have never seen anything like it." The two men he was hunting with, Mister Sawerst and Mister Cleaver, both from the upper New Hampshire area, claimed to have also seen this beast.*

*"It rose up on hind legs, walked like a man," said Mister Cleaver. "It had a big shaggy head and moved through the woods real quiet."*

*The men were uninjured and submitted this photo (at left), as evidence of the creature in the woods that they encountered. Made more sensational, is the fact that this is the same area where a local man, Mister James Smithfield, disappeared more than ten years ago. Prior disappearances in this area have been noted as well in previous years.*

Jane bit her lip, uncapped her pen, and started to write on the cheap paper.

*In the event of my demise, I, Jane Rogers, being of sound mind and body do write these words as honest truth. Before my God and my family and friends, I do swear to the validity of what I am about to record here…*

JANE HAD GROWN UP IN a large family in the country. Her father, the county's only doctor, had been gone a lot of the time, out on calls. When she was old enough, Jane used to ride with him sometimes, act as his nurse in a pinch when he had an especially tricky delivery or when the wounds from an accident had turned out to be worse than he'd anticipated.

Whenever he had free time though, her father liked to get out in the mountains. He'd been a man who threw himself completely into his passions. Medicine, of course. Work always came first. But he'd been passionate about nature too and had taught all his children about being in wild places. What plants one could find for food and which to avoid? How to make fire without matches. How to build temporary structures and how to do very basic emergency medical procedures when a doctor was miles away.

Jane wished she and Paul had spent more time in the woods themselves. When they'd first met, they'd frequently pack up picnics and hike to waterfalls or stay overnight in little, rustic cabins. But with busy jobs, it was hard to take the time to get outdoors as much as they'd like.

Now, she stood drenched in the pelting rain. Jane wished that she was anywhere but in nature. She imagined what she and Paul would normally be doing on a Sunday morning: a long, slow morning in bed, then breakfast and strong coffee and reading the newspapers. She'd attend church service in the late morning while Paul walked to the local pub to enjoy a beer before the busy workweek began again.

She shook the idea of their sunlight-flooded kitchen from her mind and pulled her collar tighter to her neck. She looked for a branch that was long enough and sturdy enough to help support Paul's weight. It had to be straight, too. In the driving rain, it was hard to see. Still, the air was like heaven after the moist denseness of the cave's air.

There was a noise—a woman's scream?—and Jane paused to listen. Had it been human? Or the screech of the wind? The gale was even stronger now, whipping Jane's wet hair into her eyes and stinging her face. What if it was Deidre? The thought made Jane's insides cold. She hated to think of her friend out here—in this freezing, wretched storm—all alone. Had Deidre found Allan before Jane? Perhaps she'd been in shock, run off into the woods. Or did she not yet know about...

The image of the swinging body filled her mind again. Jane turned quickly and headed back toward the cave. She and Paul would find a good stick to use as a crutch once they were on their way. She shouldn't leave him alone too long.

Paul's eyes were glassed over when Jane returned to the cave. He was staring up at the ceiling again and she could hear him humming in the back of his throat. She didn't recognize the tune but it made her skin break out in a fresh batch of gooseflesh.

"Paul?" she moved closer, putting a hand on his forehead again. His skin was still cool and his eyes didn't blink when she brought her hand close. He seemed in a daze or a trance. She snapped her fingers near his face but even that didn't bring a response.

The coffee pot was burbling and Jane bent to remove it from the fire. A strong hand clamped hard over her shoulder and she let out a small gasp.

"You startled me," she said, her voice calmer than she felt. "What's the matter?" She looked toward her husband. His eyes stared at her blankly, not really seeing her.

"I've been so foolish," his voice was low, barely audible.

Relief flooded Jane's body. "Oh, it's all right, darling. This is a horrible situation. Once we get you out of here and to a hospital, you'll feel—"

"I've been so foolish for so long," he whispered, his eyes focused on the black cave wall behind Jane. She could hear a scratching sound that set her teeth on edge. She wanted to turn, see what it was but her gaze was transfixed on her husband.

"I didn't realize how much I needed to be free of all of you. You're holding me back. You and Allan and Deidre. I can't keep going like this any longer. Now that I know the truth—"

"Shut up, Paul!" Jane yelled, her anger overcoming the fear twisting in her chest. "Stop this. You don't know what you're saying. This isn't you—"

"It is me. I'm the only one who can change things. Allan's dead—he got what he deserved. I hope Deidre will too. And you," he swung his strange, dead gaze toward her. "You must too. I'm going to kill you, Jane." The words were so matter-of-fact that Jane gaped in response, no words coming to her. "I have to, you see. To make things right...to be free. It will be better then—"

Jane slapped Paul hard across the face. He jerked and then his hand shot out and he backhanded her sharply on her cheek. Her head snapped back and the weight of her body toppled her over. She lay there a moment, hand under her side, trying to get her bearings. Paul seemed to forget about her. He was motionless, his gaze once again on the ceiling. She closed her eyes for a moment, then pushed herself up, scooting backward as far from her husband as she could get.

She heard and felt the letter she'd started under her right hand. She pulled it onto her lap and glanced down. Words filled the empty portion of the page, where her own had stopped. They had started off mimicking her curling script but had degenerated into mere slashes toward the end of the page.

No, not words. Rather, a single word, repeated over and over.

Kill.

Jane heard a strange, soft moaning sound. It took several full seconds to realize it was coming from her own throat.

She glanced toward Paul. He was breathing strangely, the air coming and going from his lungs in small gasps. Almost as though he were panting. He seemed to feel her eyes on him and he stood, limping toward her. He grabbed her wrist, holding it in an iron grip, and jerked her to a standing position. The letter fell to the floor.

"Paul! Paul stop it. Stop it. Let go of me right now," Jane yelled directly into his face. He blinked once and for a few seconds, his eyes cleared.

"We have to get you out of here. Away from—from that." Jane glanced at the ceiling. The symbols seemed to be moving overhead now, turning like a carousel. She blinked, shook her head, and looked away. The skittering, grating sound was growing louder. Jane looked finally toward the corner of the cave where the sound was coming from. Her breath snagged in her chest. Black mist or fog was peeling off the cave's walls. Tendrils of it—like a snake—slithered toward them.

# Chapter Seventeen

*Paul Rogers*
*Monday, November 12, 1917*
*Shiny Creek Trail*

SNOWFLAKES, FAT AND thick, were falling. Paul and Jane had stopped to adjust the makeshift splint on his arm—a gasping, horrible procedure—and rested for a moment longer on the log. They hadn't talked much since leaving the cave. Now, they watched the puffy flakes drift lazily down from the gunmetal sky overhead.

The forest was nearly silent. There was an occasional creak or squeak of a tree branch, the sporadic call of a bird. But the rest of the forest was muffled by the snow and the dense layer of dead leaves underfoot. The air smelled cold: of snow and decaying leaves and bitterly frosty fresh air.

Paul shivered and glanced at Jane. She was hunched on the makeshift bench next to him, her coat drawn as tightly as she could get it. He could see her jaw clenching as she tried to keep her teeth from chattering.

"We should go," Paul said. "It's only going to get colder the longer we're not moving."

Jane nodded, stood, and offered Paul her arm. He gave her a half hug and nodded to her. "You lead the sway. It shouldn't be long now."

But the truth was, it might be a very long time before they found their way down. With the leaves off the trees and underfoot, and everything coated in a blanket of white it was becoming harder to make out the trail. Paul's footsteps from days ago were long gone. The Green Mountain Club had been working for several years now to add blazes—strips of paint—to the trees on the Long Trail, this area hadn't yet been tended to. If only he had his compass. A map. Or some morphine.

Paul grimaced. The fiery pounding in his shoulder had been reduced to an incredibly hot, sharp pain whenever it was jostled. And maneuvering the rocks and slippery leaves and snow underfoot made immobilizing his arm impossible.

Jane slid down a hidden rock face in front of him and fell.

"Are you all right?" Paul rushed forward, ignoring the throbbing, bleating pain.

Jane stood slowly and dusted herself off. "I'm fine."

"Maybe I should take over the lead. If I fall it's not so bad—"

"No, Paul. You're injured. If you fall we could be in even worse trouble than we already are." Jane sounded tired. Paul shook his head. She had to be exhausted. He worried too, that seeing Deidre's body had drained the rest of the spark from Jane. She hadn't spoken much since then, not that he'd been a great conversationalist.

"Come on. Let's keep going," she said. "How is your arm holding up?"

"Fine."

They trudged onward. At least they were going downhill. Sooner or later they'd come out of the woods and find the road. And people. A town. A hospital. Food and warmth. The images of a syringe of numbing medicine and a mug of steaming coffee did battle in Paul's mind.

He bit the inside of his cheek as he misstepped and bumped his bad arm into a tree. A plop of snow fell onto his head. This whole situation might be comical if it wasn't so unnerving and painful.

Jane had stopped when he did and studied him as he brushed the snow from his head, seeming to read his mind. "I feel like we're in a comic strip. Only a really bad one where everything goes wrong."

She really was flagging. Jane was the eternal optimist.

Paul nodded as they started walking again. "Yeah," he said, trying to inject energy into his voice. "But it won't be much longer. Every step is bringing us closer to town. It won't—"

Paul stopped as he heard an unfamiliar sound above and to his left. He turned to look. This part of the trail was deeply wooded, with huge, craggy boulders nestled into the side of the mountain. Small trees, lichen, and moss grew out of the rich soil on these large stones. Above them—maybe fifty feet away—was a large, flat ledge. It rose from the largest boulder and was crested with another large boulder wedged into the side of the mountain. It created an overhang. It would be a perfect place to spend the night, a built-in lean-to.

But as Paul looked more closely, he saw something that made his heart stumble before it smashed hard into his ribcage. A large, dark shape stood on the ledge. It was partially hidden by the shadows cast by the overhang, but Paul could see the shaggy form, the black snout.

"Jane." His voice was barely more than a whisper. "Jane." He repeated it more loudly when she didn't turn around.

She stopped, glanced back over her shoulder.

"There's a bear above us. On the ledge to my left. Don't panic."

But panic was already washing over Paul. He tried to remember facts about bears in Vermont. Black bears. Small to medium in size compared to say, grizzlies. Not often aggressive except when very hungry or with young cubs. But now? In mid-November, shouldn't it be hibernating? It had to have been the dry fall they'd had. It had dried up the berries, maybe it had also changed the bears' hunting patterns if prey had to look for water in other places.

Jane swallowed. Her eyes were wide and fixed on the bear.

"What should we do?" Her voice was a stage whisper.

Paul shook his head. "Keep walking. Let's just try to go a little faster. I don't think it would attack us."

"Should we make noise? Aren't you supposed to wear bells on your clothes around bears? They're more frightened of us than we are of them, aren't they?" Jane's voice was soft, pleading.

"Yes. Yes, I'm sure you're right. But since it might not have seen us yet, let's just keep going. Better not to draw attention to ourselves, than to—"

Paul's voice broke off. He and Jane stood transfixed as the bear rose on its hind legs, sniffed the air delicately. It was surprisingly graceful for having such a roly-poly body. Then it turned its large, shaggy head in their direction.

They'd been spotted.

"Go," Paul said. "Move now, Jane."

She stumbled forward at a half jog, Paul right on her heels. He tried to listen to the sound of a large animal crashing through the undergrowth, but the sound of their feet pounding over the stones and rustling half-dried leaves and their breath coming in ragged clouds made it difficult. Paul glanced over his shoulder. He couldn't see anything moving.

They went as fast as possible, using branches and trees occasionally when the leaves underfoot slipped. Above, the sky was lightening slightly, the fat snowflakes falling slower. Paul listened for sounds of huffing breath, of breaking branches, but couldn't hear any. They were going to be all right. Maybe the bear hadn't seen them after all, or didn't want to exert the energy of trying to—

A roar sounded behind them. Paul had heard the expression, "froze my blood," more than once. Now he understood it. Ice coursed through his veins. Ahead of him, Jane let out a gasp of fear. She'd turned. All the strain from the past several weeks was replaced by terror.

She yelled, "Paul, look out!"

He ducked and turned at the same time, his injured arm bashing painfully into a sapling. The bear was three yards away from them now. Two? Its body hurled toward them. Paul didn't have time to think. Instinctively, he swung the makeshift crutch out toward the bear and roared back at it. The bear halted, jerking back on its padded feet. It looked warily at Paul, snorted softly, and then sniffed the air again. Steam rose from its nostrils.

"Get out of here!" Paul yelled. The sound echoed around the woods. *Here, here, here,* the word bounced from nearby trees back at him. For a moment, everything in the world stopped. The forest was silent. The earth beneath them seemed to fade away. It was just Paul and the creature, staring at one another.

It would go, Paul realized. It would leave and he and Jane would be safe. It was—

The bear lunged forward.

Its growl seemed to shake the ground beneath them, feet pounded toward him. Paul yelled again, raised his arm, and swung the large branch at the bear. It grabbed the end and yanked it from Paul's hand. Tossed it aside. Snapped its teeth so close to his face that Paul felt its hot breath coat his cheeks.

Jane screamed.

The bear glanced away for a second, looking toward her.

"No!" Paul yelled. "Don't you touch her. Get away from here. Away, bear!" He waved his arms toward it.

The bear lunged toward him again. He sidestepped, desperate to stay out of range of the sharp, snapping teeth. It roared, causing Paul's insides to roll. His sore knee gave out as he rolled his ankle on something—branch or stone—and then Paul went down. The bear grunted and rushed toward him, toward his face. Instinctively, Paul raised his arm. He heard Jane scream again, the sound piercing the sky. Fire, like he'd been branded with a hot poker, ran down his forearm. He yelled. The bear jerked its head once to the right and Paul felt his body lift off the ground. Seconds later it slammed into a downed tree. There was no breath in his body. He stared in hopeless terror as the bear took a few steps closer. The trees around it swum dizzyingly into and out of focus.

Then the world went black.

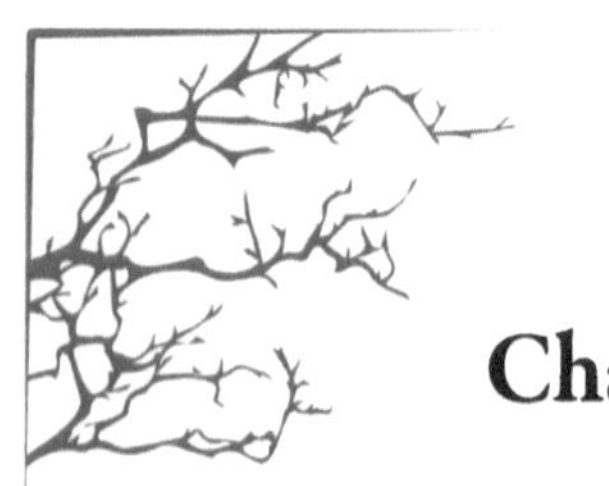

# Chapter Eighteen

*Jane Rogers*
*Sunday, September 9, 1917*
*Shiny Creek Trail*

BLACK MIST OR FOG WAS peeling off the cave's walls. Tendrils of it—snakelike—slithered toward them. Wrenching her wrist free, Jane ran to Paul's backpack. He wasn't a religious man but he might have brought it anyway. Please, please let him have brought it anyway.

She searched through the pockets of the pack and then finally in frustration dumped it upside down. She shook it: a mixture of pots, pans, the small first aid kit—already depleted—extra sweater, canteen, a notebook, two pencils, and at the bottom the camera fell out. She felt around in the interior pocket and then, finally, her hand closed over what she'd been looking for. It was a cross on a leather strap. She'd given it to him months ago. Even though he'd never worn it, she'd seen it in his pocket when she did laundry and had found it most Saturday mornings on his bedside table.

She unwound the leather strap now from around the cross and approached her husband. He was sitting propped against a large stone, his head back, gaze once again focused on the ceiling of the cave. He was humming again. She moved behind him and slipped the leather cord gently around his neck. The little cross glittered in the firelight, resting in the hollow at the base of Paul's neck. They sat in silence.

Jane prayed for a miracle, for protection, for help.

Five minutes passed. Then ten.

Finally, "Jane?" Paul's voice was small and sounded unsteady. "Jane, do we have anything else for the pain? My leg feels like a giant toothache.

Relief flooded Jane's body and she wrapped her arms around his neck and kissed it. "Yes. I'll find something. And then we need to go."

"Go?" He sounded tired. She glanced over and saw his eyes were closed.

"We need to get out of here. Leave and go find help. Find the authorities so that they can look for Deidre."

"Mmm," Paul said, his chin nearly touching his chest. His breathing was still erratic but had slowed.

A HURRICANE HAD TOUCHED down in Massachusetts the year before. Jane remembered the days of rain and high winds that had blown themselves out as they'd moved across Vermont. It had left some damage but more wagging tongues in its wake. The "great storm," was all anyone talked about for weeks.

A crack of thunder split the sky overhead and Jane jumped involuntarily. Paul who was leaning on her heavily squinted his eyes and peered at her. Rain slashed at their faces. It had instantly drenched them. A glance upward now revealed thick, rolling black clouds. She could smell something charred—a tree hit by lightning?—and urged her husband forward.

"Almost there now, Paul," she reassured, more for herself than him. He was feverish, his skin hot against hers even through the layers of clothes, they wore. "It won't be long. We're nearly to the trail."

The wind writhed and howled around them like a living thing. It snatched at their clothes, their hair. It screamed and tore leaves, showering them down on Jane and Paul. She stumbled and put her hands out as rain slashed over her face, in her eyes. Paul's arm started to slip from her shoulders and she overcorrected, dragging him so far in the other direction that they both nearly toppled over.

"I've got you," she said. The wind instantly snatched the words away.

This was foolish. Ridiculous. They should wait until the rain stopped...and yet, even as Jane thought the words her heart lurched. The storm outside was nothing compared to whatever was in that cave. She'd gamble on Mother Nature over the supernatural any day of the week.

The trail had to be close. She'd wanted to come out first by herself, mark a path to Shiny Creek Trail from the cave. Then go back for Paul. But realization had dawned: Paul couldn't stay in that cave any longer. His fever had started soon after they'd finished a pot of oatmeal.

She'd checked his leg again, gently peeling back the makeshift bandage and using the last of the cream and the solitary fresh cloth from the first aid kit to dress the wound. It had looked angry and red and her ministrations had made it start to bleed again. She'd noticed Paul's face then—red and hot to the touch—and his bleary-eyed gaze. Still, even that was a relief compared to the other behavior...

Another crack of thunder nearby startled Jane back to the present. Was it this downed tree that the foursome had climbed over on their way to the cave? Jane stopped, bit her lip, and looked behind her. Faintly, she could see the undulating strip of fabric that she'd tied to a bush. Every twenty yards or so, she left another, knotting them tightly so that they wouldn't be yanked off by the stiff, grasping fingers of the wind.

She frowned and studied the fallen tree. It was large. She thought she remembered it. Jane longed to ask Paul, but of course, he wouldn't remember. She marked one of its broken branches with another fabric strip. The wood was slick and smelled earthy and dank. She leaned Paul against the rough trunk and scrambled over the tree. When she glanced back, her husband was gone.

"Paul?" her voice cried out in the wind. She retraced her uncomfortable steps back over the tree. It was wide and she had to shimmy and scoot her way over the large, wet trunk on hands and knees.

He lay on the other side of the trunk, flopped like a discarded rag doll on the earth beside it.

"Oh, Paul. I'm so sorry." She jerked her leg impatiently over a branch that had snapped off. Tears filled her eyes as the jagged wood ripped her pantaloons and scraped her skin raw underneath.

She pushed and pulled Paul into a sitting position, his back against the fallen tree. Then she sat next to him, pressing her own back into the wet wood.

She couldn't do this. She wasn't going to be able to get him down the trail. Even if she could find it. Not like this. He could barely walk. She was so tired. Her limbs ached and trembled, her fingers were numb with cold. She looked at her hands. The fingertips were lavender and the skin was pruned from the rain.

*Please, please help me.*

Paul's teeth were chattering. She moved closer, ran her hands up and down his arms, trying to bring some warmth to him. It was useless though. Their clothes and boots had long ago been drenched. Rainwater ran in rivulets down her neck and into her sodden blouse. Itchy streams cascaded down her face, dripped from her nose, and blurred her vision.

Jane put her head on Paul's shoulder. She was so tired. Maybe if she rested, just a few minutes—

A noise sounded in the trees nearby. Jane lifted her head, but everything was blurry. She rubbed a hand over her face again, clearing the rain away so she could see.

Something moved in the forest nearby.

"Deidre?" She shouted before thinking. "Deidre, is that you?"

She searched the limp leaves, the undulating undergrowth but there was no flash of color, no answering reply.

She glanced toward Paul, then froze. About twenty feet away stood the creature. The same one she'd seen that night with Deidre. She had heard its huffing breath just the day before when she'd been in the forest outside the cave.

Panicky fear skittered up her backbone. Icy fingers of anxiety squeezed her chest. Jane sat, motionless.

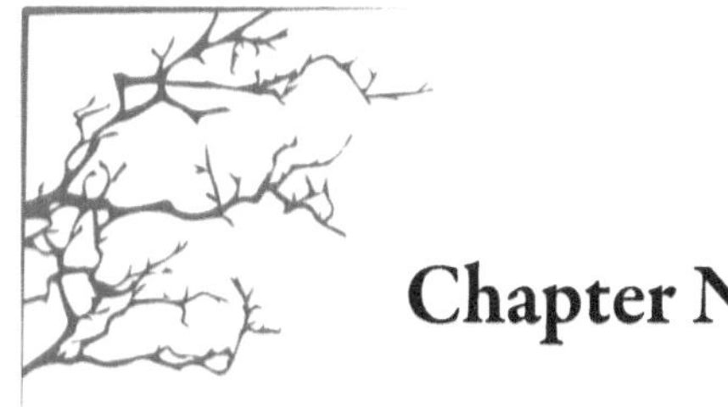

# Chapter Nineteen

*Paul Rogers*
*Monday, November 12, 1917*
*Shiny Creek Trail*

SOMEONE WAS USING A jackhammer outside of his window. That was Paul's first thought before he opened his eyes. The second was that he'd been run over by a train. His eyelids fluttered. The sky and trees above him whirled once, then twice before he closed them again. He moaned, turned on his side, and was sick. Hot, sour vomit pooled somewhere near his head. He blacked out again.

The next time Paul opened his eyes, he was staring at a fat, gray squirrel. It watched him from its perch on a nearby log. Its bushy tail swished and its clear, black eyes inspected him while it sniffed the air. Then it ran off, skittering through the undergrowth and leaves, leaving small footprints in the clean snow.

More flakes were falling. They covered Paul's face gently. He lay like that for a long time, just breathing, testing his injuries before he looked at them.

An explosion of pain ricocheted as he moved his dislocated shoulder—he'd landed on his back or moved onto it instinctively while unconscious. A new, burning pain erupted in his other arm, the good one, as he tried and failed to push himself to a sitting position.

Then he remembered.

The bear.

Jane.

"Jane!" he yelled, but the word came out as a whisper.

All around him, the world wobbled as he sat up. Slowly, the trees and sky went back into their regular positions. His arm throbbed in rhythm with his heart. It felt as though someone had tightened a series of gouging metal bands over it and twisted. Something warm was dripping from it. Blood, it must be. But Paul didn't look. Couldn't look.

He had to find her.

"Jane. Jane?" His whispered words tangled in the snowflakes swirling around him.

The air was cold but Paul filled his lungs with it, trying to lift the fog in his mind, to think more clearly. Little starbursts floated around the edge of his vision. He shook his head slowly, trying to clear it.

They'd been on the trail and seen the bear. It had charged them—charged him—and he'd used the stick at first to try to ward it off. Then—had he left the path before it had grabbed him, or was he still on it? Had Jane run? Please, please, let Jane have gotten away. He remembered with sickening clarity then, her face, her scream on the path as the bear had attacked.

Carefully, slowly, Paul stood. He tentatively explored his arm—the one the bear had grabbed—and his stiff fingers touched stiff, hard cloth. He glanced down. Blood had soaked through the fabric. Underneath it, he could see loose skin, muscle or fat—something whitish-pink like uncooked chicken. Dizziness washed over him. He shouldn't have looked. Fresh blood came from the openings but it seemed to be slowing. Most of it had dried. The cold air and the snow he'd been laying on had probably helped.

The snow. That gave Paul an idea. He leaned down carefully and awkwardly scooped up a large handful. He used his side to press it over the wounds in his arm, gritting his teeth as he did so. Keeping it cold would slow the bleeding.

He turned, trying to get his bearings.

"Jane," his voice again a mere whisper. "Jane, I'm coming."

Paul walked for ten minutes before he realized he'd simply made a circle. He came again to the place where he'd woken, a trail of blood barely visible in the fluffy, fresh snow. He couldn't find their tracks—his or Jane's or the bear's—and wanted to scream in frustration. But it would take too much effort.

It was strange but the longer he was here, in the woods, the more complacent he was becoming. It was the cold, he knew that on some level. But why did it matter really? He was going to die out here. So was Jane, if she wasn't already. So was their baby—

No.

He would not give in. He'd keep looking. He'd find Jane, kill the bear with his own hands if he had to. It wouldn't have his wife and child. He'd die before he let that happen.

Perhaps because of the new energy in his bloodstream or maybe because of the movement he was exerting, Paul felt warmer. He wished again that he had his compass. Still, there was the sun. He looked up expecting to see nothing above but the gray clouds spitting out white snow. But between the clouds were rays of buttery-yellow sunshine. It was unusual to see it shining at the same time it was snowing. Paul was grateful.

He forced his dulled mind to work. They had hiked in on Shiny Creek Trail going mostly northeast from the parking area. So, if he followed the trajectory of the sun, he'd be heading west. And that should lead him eventually toward the trail. Unless he was further away from it than he realized. Had the bear dragged him off the trail after he'd lost consciousness? And why hadn't it finished him off? Paul pushed away the most probable reason: that the bear had gone after Jane instead.

Chills shook his frame. He wasn't doing any good standing there, getting colder. He wiped his dripping nose on his hand and broke off the branch nearest to him. He continued on that way, checking the sun periodically and snapping off a branch every few feet. At least this time he wouldn't be walking in a circle.

"Jane? Jane, can you hear me?" He repeated the words over and over, a sort of mantra. His voice alternated from hoarse whisper to dull monotone and back again. His throat was raw and ached, his head felt thick and swollen, as though someone had stuffed it full of sheep's wool.

He had to stop every few hundred feet and lean against a tree. The blood from his arm continued oozing, and he repacked it with snow, pressing a thick layer between his sleeve and skin. He'd probably end up with frostbite, but that had to be worse than bleeding to death. Dizziness engulfed him.

Anger rose up in his chest and throat. He wanted to pound on the rough trees with his hands, to yell and smash something. He was so weak. So helpless.

He pushed off the tree and broke a nearby branch. Took five more steps.

Stopped.

Something was different here. It took a moment for him to realize what it was. The landscape looked the same: vertical, wooded, snow everywhere. But something was different. To Paul's left was something that hadn't been there seconds before. A cut in the line of trees and a slight depression in the ground under the snow.

He'd found the trail.

He followed it down, his pace still too slow. He called to his wife again and again but her name was muffled by the thick snow. He'd paused to rest against another tree, this one still had most of its dry leaves, when he saw it. A smear of red on the leaves in the undergrowth. Paul bent closer, steadying himself on the tree's trunk.

Blood.

He looked around him, carefully inspecting the rest of the area. At first, he didn't see anything. Just snow-covered branches and thick, puffy rocks and downed stumps that looked like white pillows.

But then...another spot of blood. A bush about six feet away had more of it. Nearby other bushes and low-hanging branches were snapped, some broken, some dangling. Something had happened here. A struggle.

His heartbeat throbbing in his head, Paul followed the broken branches. He started to call out to Jane again but stopped himself. What if she were cornered by the bear? Surprise would be his best bet. He found a thick, hard branch—it was still green, probably fallen in the storm—and hefted it in his hand. He kept his eyes on the brush, looking for more signs of blood or broken branches.

There!

Another patch of branches, half-flattened. And there were depressions in the snow, where maybe underneath footprints lay. He moved on. Before him was a large outcropping of boulders. Most of the stone faces were covered in bright green moss. He heard a noise and stopped.

What was it?

The wind stirred the branches overhead and the sound of rattling leaves whispered. But there had been something else...

He hurried forward, toward the stones. Another smear of blood on some low-lying leaves. When he rounded the bank of rock, he saw it.

The bear was near the boulders. It was sleeping there. Its back was covered in a light sheet of snow. Paul looked around wildly. Where was Jane? He refocused on the bear, crept closer. He raised the branch in his hand. Crept forward, his feet soundless in the snow. His arm shook and he felt fresh warmth track down under the soaked shirt sleeve.

Closer.

A few more steps.

Then he saw Jane.

She was lying underneath the bear. Her eyes were closed. The bear's bulk completely covered her body with only her head sticking out. Her face was as white as the snow that was partially covering it.

Jane. Jane?

She was dead.

Jane had been killed by the bear.

Paul yelled and brought the branch down with all his strength on the bear's large, shaggy head. He heard it crack against the creature's skull, felt flames of pain race down his arm. He ignored it and hit the bear again and again and again. He yelled and grunted. It had killed her. Had killed beautiful, kind, Jane. It had—

"P...Paul?"

He thought he'd imagined the whisper of his name. He raised his arm to bring down the branch again, only realizing now that the bear hadn't moved once since he's started hitting it.

He looked at Jane. Her eyes were open but she looked dazed.

Paul rushed to her side, throwing the branch down as he did so.

"You're alive?" he barely got the words out before he started to sob. Putting a hand to her face, he stroked her cheek, then bent down and kissed her face—her forehead, cheeks, nose, her mouth. "You're alive, Jane?"

She smiled wanly. "It...would seem...so. I..."

Her eyelids fluttered closed again.

"Jane?" Panic crept up his neck. He tried to push the bear away but it was like trying to roll a giant boulder with a toothpick. He looked at Jane. If he could hook an arm under her shoulders, perhaps he could pull her out?

He tried.

Jane's eyes flew open and she gasped. "Don't!"

"I'm sorry. I'm sorry, Jane. But I've got to get you out of here."

She whimpered. "...lost blood." Her voice was so soft that he had to lean in close to hear her. "Bear...got...me."

He swallowed. "All right. Don't worry, I'll get it off of you somehow."

She lay silently again, eyelids fluttering closed. She must be in shock. He thought it was important to keep her awake, not let her slip into unconsciousness. Right now though, he had to figure out how to get a two-hundred-pound bear off of her. He pulled his belt free from his trousers. His hand was slippery on the leather as he wound it around one of the bear's front legs. It was still warm. It hadn't been dead long then.

Suddenly a horrible thought occurred to him: what if the bear wasn't dead? What if it, like Jane, it was merely unconscious?

He looked more closely at the bear's body. It was laying with its back legs out, sprawled like the bear rug he'd seen once at Allan's parents' home. He studied the thick black fur. Its sides weren't moving. Were they? He blinked back dizziness and tried to focus his eyes.

No, it wasn't breathing he was sure. Pretty sure anyway.

Paul stood and braced himself on a nearby tree, wrapped the leather belt around his good arm twice and pulled. He pulled so hard that everything started to go gray around the edges of his vision, so hard that he felt like something was going to pop in his head.

The bear moved one inch. Then another.

Paul stopped. Sweat had broken out on his face and nausea rolled over him. He stood, panting in the cold for a minute. This would take hours. And Jane didn't have hours.

*Think. Think!*

He stood motionless, watching the snow fall down in its meandering path toward the ground. He watched it coat a nearby branch on a downed tree. Suddenly, Paul remembered something his father had taught him when he was a kid. It's easier to move something by pushing than pulling. The force used could then be his entire body weight, rather than simply the strength of his single arm. A wounded arm at that.

He looked at the bear again. Looked at the boulder behind it.
And knew what to do next.

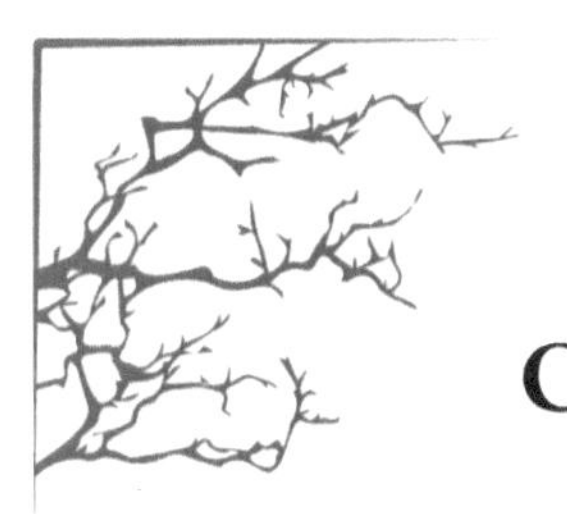

# Chapter Twenty

JANE STARED AT THE creature. Then she closed her eyes.

*This isn't real. This isn't real. This cannot be real.*

When she opened them again, the creature was still there though. It was tall—seven feet at least—and its ape-like body was covered in hair that was thick, brown and matted. Its eyes—like liquid gold—shone out from the dark face.

It looked at her but didn't move. It was so motionless in fact, it looked stuffed. As though she could walk right up to it and poke it.

Jane swallowed. "He...Hello?" Her voice was little more than a whisper. She licked her lips, tried again. "Uh, hello. Can you...can you understand me?"

The creature remained still, watching her. Its chest moved in and out, in and out. She could hear, faintly, the slight *huh-huh-huh* of its breath.

She glanced at Paul. He was shivering hard. She pushed her hair out of her eyes, wiped her face again. "Please, can you help him?"

Again, there was no motion. But its eyes looked slowly from her to Paul. It seemed to study him, then took a step closer. Jane shrank back. It stopped, looked at her again.

"I'm sorry," she said, then felt the wild desire to laugh. The wind screamed around them and she doubted the creature could even hear her, but she went on. "I'm...I'm Jane," she said, placing a hand to her chest. "This is my husband, Paul. He's...he's hurt. I need to get him to help. I need..." her voice trailed off. The creature moved closer. It paused, looked at her, then Paul again. And came closer still. Then it bent over Paul.

Every instinct in Jane said to run at it, beat against it with her fists. It would hurt Paul. She was being stupid. She couldn't trust—

But then it looked at her again.

As the golden eyes studied her an unexpected peace flowed through Jane's body. It was going to be all right. Jane didn't know how she knew this—the creature didn't speak to her or pantomime out its intentions to help—she just knew. It slid its long arms under her husband and lifted him up like a small child. It cradled Paul in his arms—her arms? Was it a male or female?—and looked again at Jane who suddenly felt warm. It was as though the yellow eyes were flames coating her in heat. She took a step backward, stumbled and looked down at the ground.

"There," she pointed toward where she thought the trail was. "I need to get him back to the town. To get him help."

She was about to ask, "do you understand what I'm saying?" but didn't. She knew that it did. Somehow, it knew.

LEAVING PAUL WAS THE hardest thing Jane had ever done. She half-expected to see her heart, flopped from her chest and pounding on the ground by the creature's feet when she turned to retrace her steps. It had looked at her for a moment, the golden eyes searching her face. Then it had turned toward the trail, back to the car and civilization.

Jane said a silent prayer and turned back, tears mingling with the rain on her face, her mouth open in a silent howl. She had to go back. Had to find Deidre, help her friend. But everything in her heart told her not to.

She wished now that she'd listened.

Jane had finally made her way back to the cave. But it was empty. All of their things—the packs, the food, canteens, first aid kit, the bedrolls—all of it, gone. At first, Jane thought she'd once again found the wrong cave. But the ashes from their fire and a small pile of kindling were still there. So were the weird drawings on the ceiling above.

She sank down on her knees by the fire, head in hands.

Who would have done this? Other hikers must have come—taking refuge from the storm just as their group had. Fiery anger rose in Jane's chest and she threw back her head and howled. Everything was gone. Everyone was gone. Allan and Paul. Deidre.

No. Deidre was here. She had to be here. Jane wiped her face, blew her nose on a sodden handkerchief in her pocket and straightened her shoulders. Deidre was somewhere nearby. She needed Jane. She needed to know if she didn't already, that Allan was...gone. And Jane pledged that she would not only find her friend but that she'd help to give Allan a proper burial. Or at least cover him until the search team came. Until help arrived.

If it arrived.

Jane straightened her clothes, smoothing a hand over her soaked pantaloons and jacket. She needed to start a fire and fast. Her teeth were chattering loudly, the anger over the theft of their belongings had faded and the temporary heat it had created in her body was replaced by bone-aching cold. Her fingertips were blueish, and she imagined her lips matched.

Flint. This she'd wisely kept in her pocket. With it and a stone, she'd have a fire burning in no time. Then, after she'd warmed herself and let her clothes dry, she'd go and find Deidre.

Her friend needed her.

# Chapter Twenty-One

*Paul Rogers*
*Monday, November 12, 1917*
*Shiny Creek Trail*

PAUL LINED UP THE THICK walking stick he'd been using directly behind the bear's shoulders. He dug the pole into the ground between the boulder and the bear. He pushed down. Blood immediately sprouted from his forearm. But the bear moved, just a couple of inches before it collapsed back down. Jane let out a little huff of breath, her eyes still closed, her face still just as pale.

He'd need to get more force on the branch in order to gain more leverage.

Paul was panting slightly as he readjusted his position. This time, he faced the pole, not the bear. With his back to the animal, he squatted deeply, winding his good arm around the pole and holding it as close to his chest as he possibly could.

He took a deep breath and pushed down with all his strength. He couldn't see behind him to know if the bear was moving—that was the downside of this position—but he heard something. He continued to push, hard then harder. Sweat popped up along his forehead and a loud groan came from his throat. The pole was near to where his waist would be if he were standing. His breath was coming in shallow gasps. Every part of him hurt but all he could think of was Jane, pinned under the bear, and the baby that she protected in her belly.

He paused, trying hard to maintain the same amount of tension on the makeshift lever, and glanced over his shoulder. The bear was lifted from the ground at least six inches, maybe eight.

"Jane!" he called out. He needed her to wake up, needed her to roll out from underneath the massive weight. "Jane," he said again, his voice fainter. His arm and legs shook, making the pole bounce and jitter.

No!

The branch slipped from his sweaty hands and landed again on the ground, covering Jane.

Paul sat on his haunches for several long minutes. Frustration pounded in his bloodstream, throbbed in his forehead.

He waited until his breathing was almost back to normal. Then he walked to Jane's face, crouched again. He hesitated a moment, then slapped her smartly across the cheek. She blinked once, twice. Then her eyelids fluttered.

"Jane?" He put his shaking hand on the small sliver of shoulder he could see and shook her gently. "I'm sorry, darling. But I need your help. I need you to—"

But her eyelids were already shutting again.

"No. Jane, no. Look at me. Wake up. I need you to listen to me right now. I can't do this on my own. You need to help me help you and the baby. Please, Jane. Please—"

Her eyelids fluttered again. When she opened her eyes this time, they remained open though she stared vacantly at him without recognition on her face.

"Jane? Can you hear me?"

No movement at first, then a slight nod.

"Good. That's good, Jane. Listen to my voice. I need you to just stay with me for a few more minutes, all right? There's something you need to do."

No reaction.

Paul hurried to explain while she was still conscious. "I found a way to hoist the bear slightly. But you need to get out when I do it, all right? Crawl, roll—whatever you need to—just get out from underneath it. Can you do that?"

Again, no reaction.

"Jane?"

Then a nod, barely perceptible. "Y..."

Her voice was little more than a whisper.

"Good. Good, Jane. I'm going to get into position now. Then I'll count to three. When I hit three, you move, all right?"

"Mmm," Jane said, her eyelids fluttering again.

"No, stay with me please, Jane."

Paul patted her cheek a few more times then hurried back into position. He took as deep a squat as possible. Felt his muscles tighten and fire and pain radiate everywhere as he started to push down on the branch.

"One..." he panted. "Two..." His legs and arms shook. Paul mustered all the strength he had left and shouted, "Three!"

He felt something shifting on the other end of the pole—prayed that it wasn't the bear sliding off—and then heard another sound. Something scraping along the ground, rustling the leaves. Jane was moving. Please, please let it be Jane moving.

The edges of his vision were turning gray.

"...free." He thought he imagined the word at first. But as he collapsed once more on the boulder he glanced back. Jane's body lay crumpled beside the bear's head. She'd done it. They'd done it. He wanted to whoop, throw a fist into the air overhead but couldn't find the energy to even smile. Paul made his way to Jane. It wasn't until he'd rounded the bear, squatted down beside Jane that he saw the extent of her injury.

Blood covered the front of her. There was so much of it. Her jacket and blouse were stained dark maroon. Fresh blood oozed from her right shoulder. Paul looked more closely. There was something very wrong with that. He groaned, his hand covering his mouth. The top of Jane's shoulder had been mauled. Where before it had been a sturdy, rounded curve, now there was a mess of blood and tissue and bone. It was impossible to tell that it had ever been a shoulder or even part of the human body. The smell of blood was thick in the air. Jane's eyes were closed again, her face even whiter—if that were possible—than before.

Was she...?

"Jane?" Paul smoothed her hair away from her face. "Jane?" He bent close, pressed his ear to her nose and mouth. He couldn't feel anything, but his face felt numb with cold.

"Jane!" he shouted. He stopped and watched her chest. Yes, there. Barely moving but moving.

Think, Paul. He had to stop the blood. How much had she already lost? He looked around him but there was nothing to use. His fingers fumbled as they tried to unbutton his shirt. Finally, in disgust, he pulled hard. Pain shot from his dislocated shoulder and he slowed for a moment, easing it over the spot. Then he tilted Jane on her side, wound the shirt over and over the wound. Sitting back on his heels, Paul felt a sob building in his throat.

What were they going to do?

Shivers ran through his body as he contemplated their options. He could try to get Jane back under the bear—at least she'd be warm—and go for help. Immediately, he discarded the thought. He wasn't leaving her, not again. What then?

He looked at her still form.

"In sickness and in health. Till death do us part," he whispered, leaning down over her still body. "Remember that, Jane?"

Silence.

Paul looked again at the bear. How had his wife—a fraction of the size of the black bear—managed to kill it? The animal was slumped half on its side now, the branch still propped underneath its chest where Paul had left it. He walked to the other side, looked down.

The knife from the cave was buried deep into the bear's chest. Jane had plunged the blade in, up to the handle. Before or after it had gotten her shoulder? Maybe while. Paul winced, imagining the scene: Jane's screams, the bear's roar of pain, the blood spurting from her shoulder. He retrieved his walking stick-turned-bear-lever. Then he knelt in the snow beside his wife.

"We're getting out of here, Jane," he said, and with a grunt, lifted her up and over his shoulder. "One way or another."

He staggered, tried to find his balance. Jane wobbled and for one horrible moment, he thought they were going to fall over backward. But he righted himself and moved forward. Using the sturdy branch to dig deeply into the snow and undergrowth, he took first one step and then another.

# Chapter Twenty-Two

*Rory Grant*
*Friday, November 16, 1917*
*Green Mountain Gazette Office*

"WELL, I THINK IT'S absolutely the bees' knees," Juliet gushed, a slim cigarette propped in her even slimmer fingers. "What an adventure."

Rory smiled, shook his head, a laugh exiting through his nose. "I should let you talk to the source. He might change your mind."

Juliet waved a hand through the air, as though discouraging a pesky mosquito. "But think of it," she said. "Imagine the story."

"I am, Jules. That's my job."

"No, no. Not you, silly. I mean the couple—what was it again? Rogers." She smiled, satisfied to have recalled the name. "Imagine the publicity opportunities? Newspapers, journals. Why, I wouldn't be surprised if Hollywood called and wanted to make a moving picture of their story. He's a hero, Rory, you have to admit it. Everyone will want a piece of that story. Oh, I envy them! I truly do."

"Hmm," Rory said, unimpressed. "I suppose. But along with the story is all the scars they have to bear."

"Oh, pish-posh," Juliet said and sucked on the end of her cigarette. She blew circles of smoke above his head, her red, glossy lips forming a perfect "o".

"They'll heal." She spoke with the naiveté of someone whose biggest tragedy included a missed bus.

"Well not all of them," Rory said and shifted in his chair. He could practically feel the hot breath of his editor on the back of his neck from here.

"No. Well, that was unfortunate," she made her mouth turn down in an attempt at sympathy. "But still...I can't stop thinking about the story angle. Did you pose the idea of a book to him?"

Rory turned a laugh into a cough. "Er, no. We ran out of time. They're both still pretty weak. Mr. Rogers' nurse kicked me out after twenty minutes."

"Pity. Still, I'm sure that once they've fully recuperated—"

"Look, Jules. I appreciate your...interest. But I've got to get started on this story. Firth needs this by noon if it's going to run today."

"Sure, sure," Juliet said, rising from the stool she'd dragged near to Rory's desk. "I've got my own story to tackle. The annual holiday pie contest over in Weston," she wrinkled her nose, stubbed the cigarette out in the ashtray on a nearby desk. "When's Firth going to realize that I'm a crackerjack reporter and stop handing me these fluff pieces?"

"When you've been here as long as me."

Juliet laughed. "Gawd, I hope it doesn't take that long. What's it been for you now, two decades? Three?"

Rory waved a hand in her direction, his attention already focused on the typewriter in front of him, the sound of the keys drowning out everything else in the noisy newsroom.

*Young Couple Escapes Death on Shiny Creek Trail*
*Two still missing after hiking trip*

*Paul and Jane Rogers of Burlington were found by a passing motorist outside of Gaston early Tuesday morning. The couple was rushed to Haystack Hospital where they were treated for numerous serious injuries. Along with exposure and frostbite, the couple had experienced a bear attack. Mr.*

*Rogers suffered more minor injuries than his wife and spoke with this reporter today from his hospital room.*

*"It was hell, but I never doubted that we'd make it out," Mr. Rogers said.*

Rory remembered how the younger man had cradled a mug of coffee between two battered-looking hands. His arms, both bandaged, had been barely visible through his open dressing gown. Underneath, a hospital johnny had peeked out the cloth dotted with faded flowers. Paul's face had been bruised and scraped. His wife Jane though had looked even worse.

Rory and Paul had walked slowly—so slowly—to her room in the women's wing. She was still on a ventilator, swaddled in so many layers of dressing that Rory could barely make out the shape of a body within the bandages and tubes. Her face was gaunt, a tube sticking out from between pale lips.

"She was pregnant," Paul had said, his voice cracking. "That was what got her through the worst of it I think."

Rory who had three kids of his own had felt his stomach flip. He hadn't wanted to ask if she'd lost the baby. Turns out he didn't have to.

"I didn't think the baby would make it. But it did. If Jane is one thing it's persistent. I think she willed the baby to stay alive, even when she herself must have felt like dying. I didn't doubt we'd make it out so much," Paul said, his voice fading. "Only if we'd have enough left in us to go on afterward."

*Covered in bandages to protect his frostbitten skin, Mr. Rogers stated that he and his wife, along with two friends, Allan and Deidre Warning, had originally hiked Shiny Creek Trail in September of this year. After an unexpected storm hit the area, Mr. and Mrs. Rogers became separated.*

*Somehow Mr. Rogers made it out of the woods, while the others in the party did not. The couples' families had contacted authorities after they'd failed to return home from their trip.*

*In the September 11th issues of the Green Mountain Gazette, readers first learned of the harrowing hiking trip which, according to Mr. Rogers, left one person dead and two others missing. "I knew that Jane was alive," he told this reporter at today's interview. "She's so strong. I knew she'd have made it."*

*Mr. Rogers had been hospitalized back in September after being found by a hiker close to the entrance of the trailhead. Though searchers combed the Shiny Creek Trail area, they were unable to locate any of the other party members. Nor were they able to locate the cave which Mr. Rogers stated that the friends had taken refuge in.*

Rory lit a cigarette and leaned back in his chair. It squeaked in loud protest. He pondered the information he'd found when he'd done his first investigation back in September. Paul Rogers had ended up at the Vermont State Hospital for the Insane where psychologists debated his "delusional state," and "far-fetched imaginings." There had been talk about a man-beast, a Bigfoot—something Rogers had seen out in the woods. Should Rory include that bit of research in this article? Doing so would cast his source in a less-than-favorable light. But didn't readers have the right to know?

Rory had heard stories himself of something out in those woods. Something big and elusive, with shaggy hair, that stood taller than any man should. He pulled on the cigarette again, then forced the smoke out in a perfect stream like a steam engine.

He'd heard a man at a bar talk about the creature once. It had been shortly after Rory's first article had come out in September. The man had been half in the bag that night at the pub.

"I'm telling you bunch, there's something in those woods. I met this Indian girl, see? She said that place up there is," he'd paused, looked around the room. Seeing the other men's eyes focused on him, he'd sniffed, leaned back in his chair. "It's haunted. She said so herself. And her tribe's been around here for decades. Nah, longer. Probably a hundred years." He'd thrown back the rest of whatever brown liquid was in his glass.

"She said there's a man-beast, a Bigfoot, see? Hairy, tall old thing. Lives up in those mountains. Protects it like."

"Protects it from what?" a man across the table had asked, resting his elbows on the scarred pine table.

The storyteller glanced at him, then down at his empty glass. "Ain't sure. Us, maybe."

Rory hadn't been able to hear much more after that, over the catcalls and laughter of the man's friends. He'd wanted to talk to the man, had waited on his own barstool for a long time. But when the storyteller had finally stumbled out of the bar he'd leaned heavily on the arm of a buddy, eyes half-closed.

Rory took another drag on his cigarette now and inspected the glowing end. He set it down on the lip of the ashtray. He stretched his shoulders, looked at the ceiling. Then started typing again.

*While Mr. Rogers convalesced at a hospital to the north, Mrs. Rogers somehow survived the wilderness on her own for the two months until her husband found his way again to Shiny Creek Trail. Mrs. Rogers is still in very serious condition, having just come out of a coma but is expected to make a full recovery. Significant wounds, particularly to her right shoulder, however, will linger for the rest of her life.*

*"She'll survive," said Mr. Rogers when asked if he was concerned about his wife's rehabilitation. "She has a long road ahead of her, that's for sure. But I'm not worried. Jane is strong. She'll be glad that she made it. That our little family did. Even if things aren't the way they were before...it might take some time, but she'll be grateful, I think."*

Rory remembered the other man breaking down then. They'd still been standing by Mrs. Rogers' door, watching her chest move up and down under a spiderweb of tubes and wires, the pale blue blanket shuddering the only sign of life.

"It should have been me," Paul had said, angrily rubbing the back of his hand across his eyes. "I wish to God it had been."

Rory hadn't known what to say.

Paul had spoken again. "She'll never use that arm again. Never hold our baby with it. The way that the bear's teeth..." his voice faded. "Well. Doc says there was too much nerve damage. A good portion of the muscle and bone itself is gone now. She may lose the arm itself in the end. But we'll see." Paul had sniffed, stood a little straighter. "It wouldn't be the first time someone underestimated her."

*While Paul Rogers insisted after being found back in September that Allan Warning had died, a body was never recovered. Deidre Warning, according to Mr. Rogers had also survived in the forest for the past two months. Tragically, she then died in an accident, according to Mr. Rogers, as the couple tried to rescue her. Though searchers have once again combed the area off Shiny Creek Trail, her body as of yet has not been discovered.*

"Horrible thing," Paul had said, rubbing a hand over the back of his neck as he and Rory had walked back toward his room. The man's face was paler, his hand trembled slightly. "She fell. In the cave, there was an underwater brook. She was trying to get water for us and she slipped. The impact from the stone..." his voice had drifted off once again. "Well. She didn't make it."

Then they had been back at the man's room.

"Mr. Rogers, I wonder if I could ask you a sensitive question."

Paul had looked beyond Rory, at the far wall and leaned against the doorframe of his room.

"All right," his voice had been low, guarded.

"There have been some other accounts of people who've gone missing around the area of Shiny Creek Trail. Some..." Rory had struggled to find the right word, "stories of a creature in that part of the woods. Did you or Mrs. Rogers see anything like that? Anything suspicious out there?"

For a long moment, Paul Rogers had said nothing. He'd simply stared at the same spot behind Rory's head. Rory would have thought the man had fallen asleep if he wasn't standing up with his eyes open.

Finally, Paul had shaken his head slowly. "No. Nothing like that," he said. "Just the bear." He'd glanced at Rory finally, his eyes squinting slightly. "Just the bear."

Rory had nodded, shaken the man's hand gently and thanked him for his time. He'd left Paul with a slip of paper, his name and phone number scrawled across it. "In case you think of anything else," he'd said.

Paul had nodded and given him a half-smile.

"Sure," he'd said before turning and shuffling toward his hospital bed.

THE DAY AFTER THE ARTICLE came out in the paper, Rory took a long drive in the country. On the seat beside him was a map and under it, a small knapsack filled with food, a canteen of water, a flashlight and a camera.

He wasn't going to hike Shiny Creek Trail. He wasn't going to look for a strange mythical creature in the woods. He wouldn't join the now nearly defunct search attempt to locate the bodies of the Warnings. He'd just drive to the trailhead, he told himself again, hands on the steering wheel, guiding the car over the dirt road in front of him.

Just see what he might find out there in the woods.

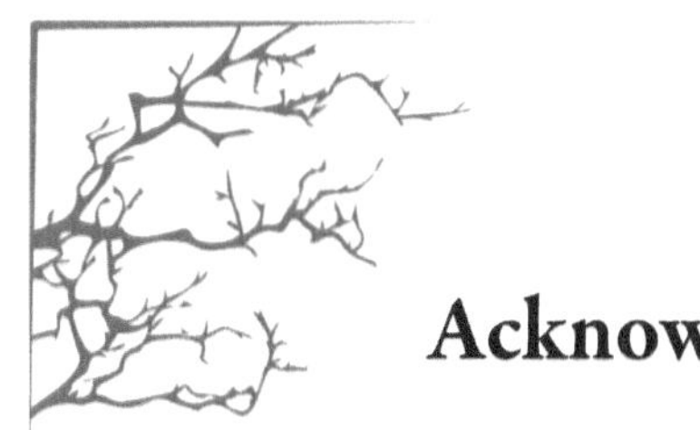

# Acknowledgments

YOU KNOW THE SAYING that it takes a village to raise a child? Well, it takes a team to write a book. To Pam Irish, Angela Lavery and Emmet Mathieu: your insights and attention to detail astounded me. Thank you for being part of the team of early readers. To Erin Chagnon: I think of you as the captain of the beta reading team. You point out things that make me laugh during editing (but would make me cry after publication), and offer great feedback and insight on things. Thank you very much for all your help and support.

Many thanks to the wonderful Helen Baggot, editor divine. I appreciate all your hard work on this project...and for not running away screaming from my overuse of commas. If there are any leftover typos, I take credit for them. Thanks also to Michele Deppe for your formatting help. You've saved me from yanking out my hair. And to Bespoke Book Covers for creating another beautiful and creepy cover.

To my readers: thank you, thank you, thank you, for coming along on another journey! Without you, there would be no point in telling these stories. I'm grateful for each and every one of you.

Lastly, for my family: my parents, sisters, in-laws, niece, nephews, uncles, aunts, cousins (whew—did I miss anyone?): thanks for your ongoing support.

My never-ending gratitude to Serge: for being steadfast and practical and also making me laugh and chill out when I need it. And to Pascal for being the sweet, silly, creative blessing you are. I love you both more than I can put into words...and that's a lot. And always, my thanks to God who has blessed me with any writing talent I have.

~Dios Amore~

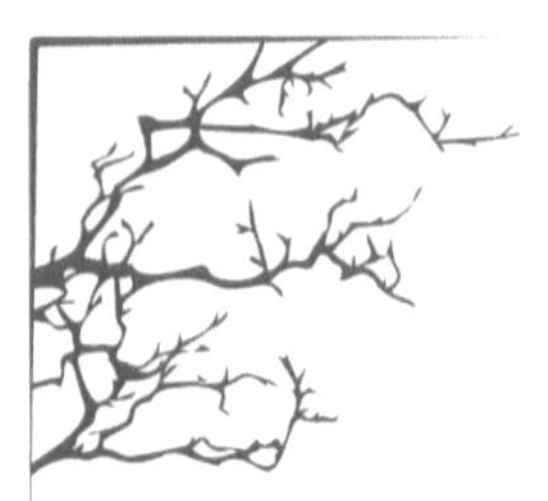

# Author's Note

I HOPE YOU ENJOYED *Silence in the Woods*, part of the "Monsters in the Green Mountains," series. Want more? Start reading the sequel, *Shadow in the Woods*, right now. I've included the first three chapters here. You can also sign up for my monthly newsletter at https://jpchoquette.me/ When you do, I'll send you a free short story.

Enjoy this bonus material and thanks for coming along on the ride.

# Bonus Material
# Shadow in the Woods

J.P. Choquette

*November 1, 1889—The Green Mountain Daily*

*Mrs. Veronica Brown of Little River seeks information on the disappearance of her daughter, Miss Lilian Brown. Widow of the late Charles Brown, an esteemed banker in the Little River area, Mrs. Brown is distraught over her fourteen-year-old daughter's disappearance.*

*Miss Brown was last seen walking on the logging road east of Little River and was wearing a red hat and brown coat.*

*Hunters in the area stated that they had seen an animal of some kind, perhaps a bear, but no evidence has been found to signify that Miss Brown met an untimely death. The local sheriff's department, along with townsfolk, have been searching the area, but no signs of the missing girl have yet been found.*

*April 17, 1971—The Green Mountain Daily*

*"It were big, I can tell you that." These words were recorded during an interview of Reginald Jarvis, a local resident of Little River. On the evening of April 16th, Jarvis states that he was walking along the logging road just outside of Little River when he saw what he calls a "Sasquatch."*

*"I never seen nothing like it in all my days on God's green earth," Mr. Jarvis stated. "It stood up on two legs just like you and me, but was covered in fur. Looked like of them big apes at the zoo."*

*Residents in the area have been warned by authorities to take additional care with their trash cans and to cease feeding birds at backyard birdfeeders. They suspect that a bear has come out of hibernation early.*

*To that Jarvis says, "Ain't never seen no bear looked like that."*

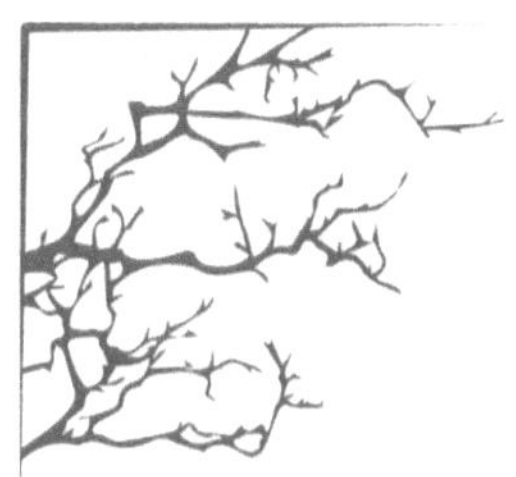

# Chapter One

MARIA RODRIGUEZ WOKE feeling as though she'd been running all night long. Her hair was tangled; a sweaty film lay across the back of her neck and knees. In her dreams, she had been running, chased once again by someone, or something, bad. When she was young her mother told her she had a sixth sense. Every morning Maria woke with this heavy twist of fear in her gut, and hoped her mother was wrong. That bad things really weren't lurking around corners waiting for her.

She rolled over, the air chilly after the sweltering blankets. Maria pushed her hair away from her face and sat on the edge of the bed, her finger pulling back the window shade. Outside, small puddles of sunlight formed on the already drying grass and piles of leaves. Vermont was beautiful in the fall and this was a day that was postcard-perfect.

For other girls, childhood had been filled with brightly colored balloons, lazy afternoons in the sun, dreaming about fairy tale endings. They had played dress up in gowns as frothy as cupcake icing, picturing themselves in Hollywood or on Broadway. Not Maria. For her, childhood was an endless maze of dark tunnels, all of the *what ifs* and *it could happens* a constant weight on her shoulders.

"Break a mirror and it's seven years of bad luck."

"Don't step on a crack or you'll break your mother's back."

"Spilling salt is a bad omen for things to come."

Maria had spent most of her childhood in perpetual worry that she would mess up. Do something careless that would ricochet its negative effects into all the years ahead of her. Or into her family's.

*Just in case* became her mantra, the worry beads her mind went to over and over again. Date rape? Better not go to the prom, just in case. Moving away after high school? College was a financial risk. Better to stay in her hometown. Get a stable but boring job, just in case she wasn't smart enough to handle something more challenging. Romantic relationships were fraught with unknowns. Better to stay single.

Maria rolled over on her side, drawing her knees up to her chest. She sighed. It was deep and heavy. "This trip is going to change your life," her therapist, Addie, had said. "Ecotherapy is a new practice to me too, but Dr. O'Dell is very familiar with it. He assures me that he's had clients who've undergone tremendous change in a short period of time. It's more popular in Europe, where counselors give clients prescriptions for time spent immersing themselves in nature. The results are astounding. You're going to break through barriers that would take us months of counseling sessions, Maria."

Now Maria looked at the alarm clocks by the bed. There were two: the one she used every morning—its annoying bleat familiar and hated—and a second one. A backup.

Just in case.

CLARK JENKINS STARTED cursing before opening his eyes. His head was pounding like a jackhammer on extra electrical current, his throat felt raw. His breath stank: a familiar brew of old cigarette smoke and sour gin. This time with an added hint of garlic.

What had he eaten for dinner? He focused on that detail. Easier to deal with than whatever had sent him on another bender. Bender. A stupid word to define getting drunk. What exactly was he bending? His opportunities?

He snorted and sat up in one motion.

Mistake.

The world spun one way and then another. He moaned for it to stop. Puking would make him feel better. Get the rest of this junk out of his system. But he didn't want to. He hated retching over the porcelain bowl, staring at the remains of the previous night. With his other hand he tentatively explored the pillow next to him.

The spinning got a tiny bit better when he found the other side of the bed empty. At least he hadn't brought Shelia or Beth home with him last night. Or anyone else. He couldn't deal with the nagging, the clutching at him, this early in the morning.

What time was it anyway? And what had woken him? Clark fumbled on the nightstand. The clock was blank, a little black bar where the numbers should be. He swore again, and checked his cell phone which he'd forgotten to plug in before he'd fallen into bed face first.

He walked to the kitchen, hand trailing his way on the wall.

Five after ten, the hands on the ugly gold face told him. What day? He leaned on the counter, willing the room to stop its orbit. Saturday. Saturday ... Saturday ... what was it he was supposed to do today? Coffee would help. His stomach burbled. Clark straightened and moved toward the pot. Then he remembered.

The trip. His counselor, Dr. O'Dell.

A string of curses rose to his lips. But the bile got there sooner. He bolted toward the bathroom.

ALASKA BAINES WAS RUNNING her heart out. At least, that's how it felt. It thumped and banged in her chest, begging her to stop, begging her to rest. What was that saying, *no rest for the wicked*? Then there was the other one, *no pain, no gain*, which pounded in her head along with the sound of her heartbeat.

Alaska was full of mantras; *try, try, try again*, and *only quitters quit*, and *there's no time like the present*. And more. Many, many more. She used mantras and sayings and proverbs and whatever else she could to motivate her team of junior ad executives. Rising to the top in the advertising department at the software firm and being a woman (doesn't being a woman always come in second?), Alaska needed all the help she could get.

It's why she did this. Running. She didn't even like it. But it served a greater purpose. Like so many things in her life—eating healthy, exercising like a mad woman, taking every personal and professional development seminar she could fit into her Type A, perfectly organized, color-coded schedule—it was necessary if she wanted to stay on top.

And Alaska did.

The trip this weekend would be a new experience for her. She'd been invited by her therapist to join the small group of clients that were going on an Ecotherapy weekend. Alaska had never been camping before, let alone backpacking. So of course, she'd said yes. It would be hard to be out of contact with work for a four-day weekend, but she'd made it work.

Feet slapping against the pavement, Alaska used a breathing technique her personal trainer had taught her to moderate her breathing. The stopwatch on her wrist told her she had three minutes to get to the mile marker if she was going to beat yesterday's record. She intended to.

*Eyes on the prize. Focus, Alaska. Focus!*

GABE SOUTHLY MOANED when his alarm clock went off, slapping at it with only one hand emerging from the cocoon of blankets. It was dark in there, and warm. He had no desire to emerge into the real world. While he drifted half-in and half-out of sleep he saw images.

People from his past flitting across the screen of his mind, but in un-usual ways. There was his favorite aunt, her lower body powerful horse's legs and she was riding a unicycle. And then the little dog they'd had as a family pet when Gabe was small appeared. It was dressed in a suit though, and when it turned its head to look at Gabe, it said, "Why do you think this is a good idea?" More images came, some humorous, some darker, all vivid.

It was this dream-wake stage that Gabe relished. That period be-tween being completely conscious and still sleeping was when his cre-ative mind flourished, feeding him images and ideas that were hard to capture in the rest of his busy day. Working as a freelance graphic de-signer wasn't at all what Gabe had pictured when he went to art school. No, he was going to be the one that stuck to his ideals, the purist who never dirtied his hand or his curriculum vitae with commercial art, who was never swayed by what a client wanted but only by his muse.

Gabe sighed and rubbed a hand over his face. His full conscious-ness was accompanied by the familiar tightness in his gut. The worries and fears always found their way to that spot and coagulated into a tight ball of stress and anxiety. Money, fame and fortune. Why was it that the things he wanted most seemed further out of reach every year?

He pushed himself up, out of the cocoon of blankets and checked the clock. He was meeting Alaska in just over an hour and still needed a shower and to finish packing his bag.

"This trip might just change your life," Dr. O'Dell had said.

Gabe had been seeing him for months now. Or was it more than a year? In fact, it was Gabe who had referred Alaska to his therapist. She was the one person he'd become friendly with at the tech company where he'd taken on some increasingly larger freelance graphic design jobs.

He yawned and pulled himself to standing. He didn't make friends, not easily, and he didn't want to let Alaska down. If nothing else, this weekend should cement the account with TriTech, something that would mean lots more business, and money, in his future.

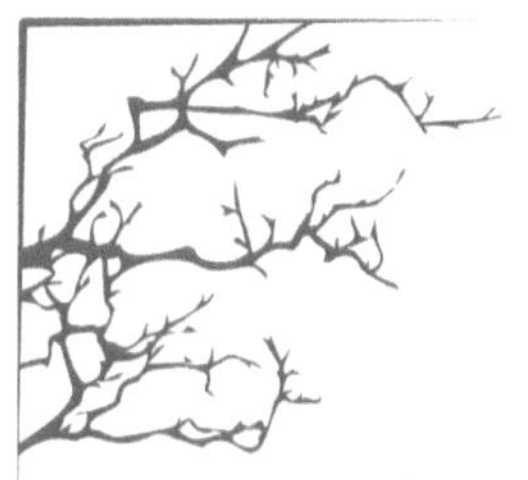

# Chapter Two

"TELL ME AGAIN WHY YOU'RE going on this trip?" Adeline Preston's son, Ben, asked. Addie stopped shoving rolled up polypropylene clothes into her backpack. She looked at her youngest. He was handsome; dark hair and eyes like his father. The only trait of Addie's he'd inherited was his nose, straight and sprinkled with freckles. She hated her own dusting but on Ben they looked charming.

At twenty-three, *he* was charming, sweet. A worrier though, even since babyhood. Ben had always looked back to check for her permission: when he was learning to walk, when he was sampling his first solid foods. Not like Michael. Three years older and miles apart in personality, the boys had never gotten along. "The Swindler," she and her ex had nicknamed Michael when he was a toddler, because he always got what he wanted, one way or another.

"It's a group therapy session," Addie said and returned to stuffing. "Dr. O'Dell and I are leading the group. It's called Ecotherapy, a sort of immersion into the natural world. It's been used in Europe for a long time. It's effective," she grunted as she pushed the final piece of clothes into the too-tight bag. "And I get a chance to see Dell, I mean, Dr. O'Dell, in his own environment."

"He lives in the woods?" Ben's voice was sarcastic.

Addie looked up and smiled. "No, but he's spent enough time there to teach me a lot about nature."

"I could teach you anything you want to know about nature, Ma." Ben made a noise of disgust in the back of his throat. "You don't even like nature."

"That's not true." Addie turned to her son again. Looking up from the floor made him seem even taller. "I love nature."

"Wildlife shows on TV don't count," Ben said. He stuffed his hands into his pockets. His corduroys were oversized and his shirt hung out over the waistband, making him appear thicker around the waist than he was.

"Here, I got you this." He pulled something from the right-hand pocket and tossed it in her direction. Addie grabbed it right before it smacked her in the face. The object was thin, cylindrical and gold-colored. It looked like a fancy tube of lipstick but when her fingers moved to where the cap should be, there was only a tiny hole.

"Careful, it's pepper spray," Ben said. "Miniaturized. It'll fit easily into the pocket on your pants."

"Thanks, but isn't it a little small to stop a bear?"

"I got you a bigger version for that," he said, handing her another cylinder. This one was red and white and screamed "STOPS" along the side. In smaller print was a miniature bulleted list of all the animals the spray would halt in their tracks: bears, snakes, wolves, mountain lions, panthers, coyotes, raccoons (!), humans.

"Raccoons? Should I be worried about those? I thought they were just greedy with leftovers." Addie laughed but Ben didn't join in.

"Rabies make any animal a danger," Ben said sounding like a professor. "The small one is for humans, just enough to surprise someone, give you a chance to get away." Ben had already reminded her several times of the attacks over the years on single women while hiking the Long Trail in the state. Addie had reminded him of the attacks that happened everywhere else. She was much more worried about animals than people.

"I'd feel better if you'd take this, too," Ben said, handing over a small pouch. It was heavier than it looked, with a nylon strap hanging from one end.

"What is it?"

"The stun gun. Look, I know you said—"

"No, Ben. Let's not talk about this again."

Ben crossed his arms, then let them hang loose, a sigh raising his shoulders up and down.

"Did you leave your itinerary somewhere?"

"Of course," she said, glad he wasn't going to start another argument about the stun gun. His concern would be sweet … if it wasn't so smothering. Instantly she felt badly for thinking like that. As a therapist, she knew the seriousness of anxiety, how it could choke a person's mind and smear their outlook with potential dangers.

While friends wouldn't define her as reckless, she'd grown up in the '70s. It wasn't all peace, love and drugs; though she'd had her fair share of those. She'd done the typical college kid thing, taken a term off school to travel around Europe. Sometimes she cringed, thinking back to the dangerous situations she'd put herself into. She'd hitched rides from strangers, gotten tipsy in bars and one night had slept on a park bench in Berlin because she couldn't remember the name of her hotel. Ben would have a heart attack if he knew. But she had refused to live life like a caged animal. That's how the American dream always felt to her: white picket fence, a dog, and a car payment.

In the end wasn't it partially that—her refusal to accept the cage, to do things the way that was expected of her—that finally broke her marriage? Ben had so much of his father in him. Too much anxiety about all that could go wrong instead of grabbing the moments as they came and letting them be what they were without trying to control every second. But it was how he was wired. While she embraced change and tried new things, these made Ben uncomfortable. She'd always worked hard as a parent to recognize his strengths: he was very smart and excelled at working with computers and troubleshooting problems, something that Addie had no patience for. And he was tender-hearted, always standing up for the underdog. The one time he'd gotten in trouble for fighting at school had been when a bigger kid was picking on a younger, smaller child. She'd given him an ice cream cone and a hug after collecting him from school, rather than a lecture.

He cleared his throat and she looked up.

"Sorry," she said. "The itinerary is on the kitchen counter by the coffee pot. Don't worry about me, Ben," she tugged on Ben's pant leg and looked up at him. "Dr. O'Dell is very capable. We're going to be fine."

Butterflies tickled her ribs but she spread a wide smile over her face. She ducked her head, hoping Ben wouldn't see. She'd be lying if she said that Dr. O'Dell himself wasn't part of the reason she was so interested in this trip. For purely professional reasons, of course.

"What are your plans for the weekend?" she asked. "Are you getting together with Lacey?"

Ben shook his head, rubbed a hand on the back of his neck. "Nah. She's busy. Well, not busy really. Just doesn't want to see me." The last part of this was muffled as Ben's hand moved from the back of his head to rub the skin on his neck and face. He scrubbed at it vigorously, then let the hand drop.

"Oh, honey, I'm sorry. I didn't know that you were having problems."

"Yeah, me either."

"Do you want to talk about it?" Addie stood, stretching her back which was aching from the position hunched over her backpack. Her legs tingled.

"Not really," Ben said, shuffling his feet. "I've gotta run some errands. What time are you leaving?"

Addie glanced at her watch.

"Dr. O'Dell is picking me up in an hour." Not Dell as she'd been calling him for the past couple of months. Like he'd asked her to. Her cheeks were getting pink and Ben frowned. His dark eyes probing, lips already parting to ask a question.

One that Addie wouldn't want to answer.

"So, I'm almost done here. Sure you won't join me for a coffee and a chat about Lacey?"

Ben shook his head, breaking eye contact. Guilt twisted her gut. *What kind of mother uses her son's love life to avoid talking about her own?*

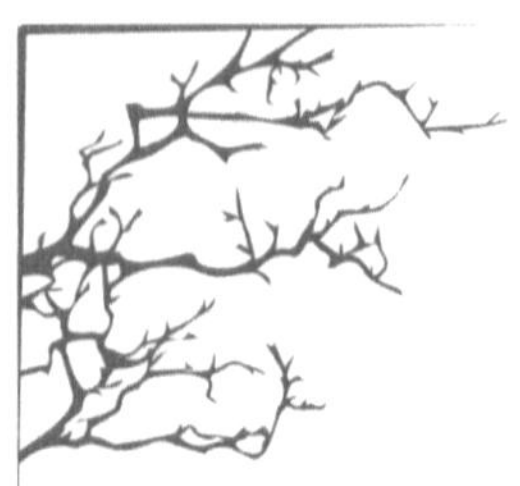

# Chapter Three

ADDIE WAS PULLING HER backpack onto the porch, holding the screen door open with her rear end to wrestle the beast out of the house when Dell's truck pulled in. It was purple and green and looked like something you'd find at a tag sale in a church basement. Her backpack, not his truck.

Glancing up mid-heave, she smiled. The truck, like the man—and probably his backpack too—was sleek and perfectly kept. Her eyes followed his progress to the porch as she stretched out of the half-crouch to her feet.

What did he see as he walked toward her? The birdhouse pole on the far side of the driveway and the lamp post in need of fresh paint. A greenish color, split-level house that could use updated siding. Overgrown flower beds tangled after a season of healthy vigor. And when had those little mounds of dirt appeared on the lawn? Another mole, likely. Addie imagined that Dell's place was a minimalist's paradise, all sleek surfaces and bare of clutter.

"Need some help with that?" Dell asked chuckling.

"I think I've got it. Might need a little help getting it into your truck through. Lifting it higher than chest-height seems dangerous."

Dell's smile widened. "Here, let me," and yanked the pack upward, slinging it over his shoulder. If he hadn't staggered slightly, calf muscles bunching, Addie would have thought he was superhuman. She pulled the front door closed tight and double-checked the lock.

"All set?" he asked, retracing his path to the idling truck. Addie nodded even though he couldn't see her. She walked down the steps and felt the many bulging pockets on her shorts and windbreaker.

Should the house key go into her pack or jacket pocket? The tiny zippered pocket over her hip or the one on the hiking vest? She'd probably forget where it was no matter where she put it.

"By nine the latest," she'd told Ben. Tuesday evening, home by nine p.m. That was the plan.

"I'll call you then," he'd replied, holding the itinerary she'd printed for him like the Holy Grail. "If you get back before, call me so I won't worry."

"I will, Ben," she'd said, hugging him hard.

"Did you forget the sink?" Dell asked now.

"What?"

"This bag weighs a ton." He grunted as he heaved the nylon pack into the rear of his truck. Addie peeked in and there was Dell's bag. Black and streamlined like she'd guessed, and no doubt perfectly packed. It had been years and years since Addie had toted her own backpack around Europe, and even then, she was constantly forgetting items behind in the hostels or leaving things behind on the train. She'd laughed to friends made along the way that it was her calling card, how they would know she was ahead of them.

"I can help you repack it when we get to the trailhead if you want," Dell offered, walking toward the driver's side. Addie climbed in the passenger seat. The truck still had a new-car smell and was warm. There wasn't a hint of dust. No food wrappers, not even a stray hair.

"My son, Ben, insists that I will need everything in it at least once." Dell raised his eyebrows.

"I'm concerned that you won't make it more than a mile, hauling that thing." Dell glanced at her for a moment before shifting the truck into reverse. Addie's cheeks warmed. Was he trying to tell her inadvertently that she was out of shape? She was, but still. While she managed to keep her weight down, she didn't embark on any of the long walks or ski trips that she'd loved in her younger years. And her thighs and biceps reminded her of this on a regular basis.

Addie turned her head, looking at Dell's profile. His eyes were dark brown and the lashes behind his round glasses were thick and dark. He had a slightly narrow face, but it lent an air of professor-ness to him. Full lips. It was odd seeing him in outdoor clothes, though. She'd grown used to the ties and vests and carefully pressed dress pants he wore at work.

"You're probably right," she said. "Taking a look at the pack before we go is a good idea."

He backed out and she caught a lemony-pine scent. His aftershave was enticing in the office and smelled even better here, in the enclosed space. She looked out the window, trying to clear her mind. *A crush on your boss is no big deal, if he doesn't know about it. Other than the discomfort it causes, of course.*

"There are mini versions of the clients' files in that accordion file behind your seat," he said. "If you want a refresher."

"Thanks." Addie stretched, seatbelt pulling at her neck and grabbed the folder, flipping through the contents.

She and Dell had been talking about the trip and the clients who would be coming for weeks now, over coffee at work, and once over lunch at *Chantal's*, a beautiful little French restaurant in town. Four clients were attending the long-weekend trip. Only one was Addie's own, Maria Rodriguez. The others were Dell's: two men and another woman. "Like a triple date," Addie had nearly blurted out when Dell had first approached her with the idea. She'd stopped herself, thank God, realizing how unprofessional the joke would be.

As the newest counselor at Maplehurst Mental Health—M&M everyone called it— she was very conscious of her status as greenhorn. "You're a natural," Dell had told her more than once, but still, Addie worried that she wouldn't fit in with the other, more experienced counselors. She'd been grateful Dell had asked her to be part of this trip. Surprised, but grateful.

"Do you have any backpacking experience?" he'd asked her then, leaning on his desk. Addie had sat in a low chair near the gas fireplace, watching Dell watch her. The clock on the wall behind her ticked loudly.

"I used to bring my boys backpacking when they were young. We did a few overnighters, but it's been a long time."

"It's like riding a bicycle," Dell had said. "It will all come back to you. Besides, the time in nature will do you good."

Addie had smiled and nodded.

It would also be great to get back into the woods. It had been too long, Dell was right. Finishing first her bachelor's and then her graduate degree as an adult student hadn't been easy. The last few years of school had stretched out even longer because she'd been working full-time between classes and papers and hours of clinical work. After she'd graduated and started working it was hard to plan hiking trips. Even weekend ones when the boys were small, felt overwhelming.

Besides, she'd needed the weekends to catch up: running errands, doing all the housework that never got done during the week. Kenneth, her ex-husband, was no help in that area. He spent most of his weekends schmoozing with prospective clients on the golf course, or flying across the country to lead sales trainings.

The file in Addie's hand tipped and the contents began to spill onto her lap. She shook herself mentally and glanced at Dell. He looked straight ahead at the road, a slight smile on his lips, humming along with a Neil Diamond song on the radio. Her palms felt a little damp against the files. She flipped open the first: a woman named Alaska Baines, mid-forties, career in PR at a tech company that Addie recognized as one of the biggest in the area. "Stress management," read Dell's neat notes under the focus of treatment area. "Reduction?" he'd noted with a question mark underneath.

The second file belonged to a man named Gabe Southly, an artist and poet who'd sought out counseling for "creative block." His file too, noted "anxiety issues" under the treatment area. Clark Jenkins was the name on the third file and Addie was surprised to see the diagnosis of anger management. She'd naturally assumed that a group session would be more effective if the clients shared similar treatment plans.

"This client, Clark," Addie said, holding a finger near the small box on the chart. "His diagnosis is the only one that's not in the realm of stress and anxiety." She looked at Dell who flashed her a smile. The wide pink lips showed white teeth beneath.

"True. Not anxious on the surface at least, but I've been working with him for some time. Although his treatment plan is for anger management and the challenging way he deals with it, underneath the frustration and rage, I sense a deep fear. You know that old saying: all humans feel only two emotions: fear and love."

"Hmm?" Addie put the file down on her lap and turned in her seat toward Dell.

"The base of every human emotion is either fear or love: hate is fueled by fear. Jealousy is fueled by fear. Compassion is fueled by love. Generosity can be fueled by either."

"Either?" Addie asked. "Generosity doesn't come from fear."

"I believe it does," Dell said, turning on the left blinker and slowing at a stop sign. "There are millionaires who give tons of money away, not out of the goodness of their hearts but because of tax breaks and loop holes and the desire, deep down—maybe even an unconscious level—to get more. They give to get."

"That's a little cynical, isn't it?"

Dell looked over at her and smiled. Her heart thumped a little harder than Addie thought necessary.

"I think like a realist," he said.

Addie looked down, flipped through the rest of Clark's chart. "So you are treating him as though he has anxiety issues, rather than anger issues?" It was an interesting concept. One she hadn't heard of before. But then there were a lot of Dell's treatment methods that were more innovative than others she'd known. Take this trip for instance. Ecotherapy wasn't new to the world of psychology, but it still wasn't mainstream by any means.

"I think it will be effective," he replied.

She read in silence for several more minutes, before the swaying of the truck on the back roads made her stomach roil. Finally, she tucked the files back where they came from and pressed her hands together between her knees.

Dell looked over at her and then back toward the road, expertly avoiding a pothole.

"Tell me ... son of a—" His hands gripped the steering wheel as though he were trying to snap it in half.

At first, Addie didn't know what was wrong. She looked at him, about to ask when she saw it. An eighteen-wheeler had drifted over the yellow dashed lines and was headed straight toward them.

Dell slammed one hand on the horn and held it there. He swerved to the right, dangerously close to the edge of a road fringed with bent and rusted guardrails. Addie's right hand scrabbled for the door handle, her left clawed at the leather seat. A scream sat behind her lips. She pulled her eyes away from the semi-trailer long enough to see the bottom of the ravine below the guardrails, far, far away.

**Order your copy of *Shadow in the Woods* now via your favorite bookseller.**

# Don't miss out!

Visit the website below and you can sign up to receive emails whenever J.P. Choquette publishes a new book. There's no charge and no obligation.

https://books2read.com/r/B-A-OQJE-GZWZ

**BOOKS 2 READ**

Connecting independent readers to independent writers.

# About the Author

J.P. Choquette is the author of suspense novels set in Vermont. Atmospheric pageturners, her novels are gothic inspired and frequently tie in the themes of art, nature, and psychology.

Her 10 novels have been downloaded nearly 25,000 times across multiple platforms.

When not writing, J.P. enjoys sipping hot drinks with a great book and adventuring with her family. She's a Believer, a vintage lover, and has never met a fruit she doesn't like.

Learn more about J.P. by visiting https://jpchoquette.me/

Read more at https://jpchoquette.me/.

9 781950 976058